The Mystery
of
Edisto Island

Other books by Idella Bodie —————————————————————

Carolina Girl: *A Writer's Beginning*

Ghost in the Capitol

Ghost Tales for Retelling

A Hunt for Life's Extras: *The Story of Archibald Rutledge*

The Man Who Loved the Flag

The Mystery of the Pirate's Treasure

The Secret Message

The Secret of Telfair Inn

South Carolina Women

Stranded!

Trouble at Star Fort

Whopper

Coming September 1999

The Revolutionary Swamp Fox

The Mystery
of
Edisto Island

by Idella Bodie

illustrated by Gay Haff Kovach

Sandlapper Publishing Co., Inc.

Copyright © 1994 Idella Bodie

Second Printing, 1999

Published by Sandlapper Publishing Co., Inc.
  Orangeburg, South Carolina

Manufactured in the United States of America
by Maple-Vail Book Manufacturing Group

Text Typeface: Palatino

Library of Congress Cataloging-in-Publication Data

Bodie, Idella.
    The mystery of Edisto Island / by Idella Bodie ; illustrated by Gay Haff Kovach.
        p.   cm.
    Summary: Phil and Jerry try to help an old fisherman on Edisto Island, South
Carolina, whose knowledge of an amazing secret threatens his life.
    ISBN 0–87844–122–0
    ISBN 0–87844–123–9 (pbk.)
    [1. Edisto Island (S.C.)—Fiction. 2. Mystery and detective stories.] I. Kovach, Gay
Haff, ill. II. Title.
PZ7.B63525Mv   1994
[Fic]—dc20   94–618
                                                                                                        CIP
                                                                                                        AC

For
Charles and Daniel,
Our Twins

Chapter 1

"There he is, Phil!" Jerry grabbed his friend's arm and pulled him back against a shed along Big Bay Creek. In his soft Southern drawl he said, "That's Gabe, the old black man I was telling you about."

Thin morning light in the dock area of Edisto Island fell over the tall, frail figure. In a shuffling kind of step, he moved around the bow of the shrimp boat. A dirty brown dog, his head low, tail under, slunk behind him.

"It's the last time I'm telling you, old man!" a gruff voice yelled. "You can't sleep on this boat."

The voice belonged to a stocky fellow, his face carved by the winds of the Atlantic. "And keep that dog off this boat too!"

"You have homeless in the South like we do in New York?" Phil asked.

"Oh, Gabe's got a home all right." Jerry rounded the corner of the maintenance shed and motioned for Phil to follow.

Nearer the tidal creek, smells and sounds of salt water swept over them. Gulls swooped and dipped over docked shrimp boats.

In a walk that seemed to move only his legs, Gabe

1

headed toward a flat-bottom boat tied to a piling at the edge of the marsh.

"He lives up Big Bay Creek," Jerry continued. "Izzie's bought fish from him forever."

"Izzie's a funny name for a grandmother," Phil said.

"Her name's Elizabeth, but I couldn't say that when I was little. It came out *Izzie* and stuck. She didn't want to be called *Grandmother* anyway." Jerry smiled. "The name fits her though. When you get to know her, you'll see."

"You're right about the old man. He's headed up the creek."

Jerry nodded. "I think his place is near the Indian Mound. It's up this creek too."

In his boat Gabe lifted his paddle from side to side, dipping it in the creek so effortlessly the boat seemed to glide along in the light morning fog. His dog's head flopped over the side.

"What I want us to find out," Jerry explained, "is why Gabe isn't sleeping at his house anymore. One morning this week I saw him hiding behind the IGA grocery store. He was mumbling to himself."

"Could you tell what he was saying?"

"Something that sounded like 'Dey attuh me' over and over."

"Do you really think somebody is after him?"

"Something's wrong. I don't know what. I feel sorry for him. He doesn't have a family. Just that dog."

"If somebody's after him, why doesn't he go to the police?"

"Oh, he wouldn't do that. The older blacks on this island are different. They believe in *boo daddies* and *plateyes*. They say these things are really dead people come back to torment the living."

"Really?"

"You wouldn't believe all the ghost stories about this island. All the old plantation houses have ghosts. Anyway, something fishy's going on. I thought you'd never get here to help me find out what it is."

Gabe had moved out of sight when Phil spoke. "Well, I think we'd better be moseying on back to the campground. Those sleepyhead sisters of ours should be up by now, and Mom should have breakfast ready."

The boys, a sharp contrast with Jerry's dark complexion and hair and Phil's red mop whorling out from a crown of cowlicks, headed toward their bicycles.

Traffic was light on Palmetto Boulevard, the main street running parallel to the Atlantic Ocean.

"Can we ride up the beach?" Phil asked. "I like to hear the sound of the waves."

"Not really. You saw it yesterday when y'all came in. Edisto has more shells on it than just about any beach you've seen. Besides, they've put that riprap out like a jetty every so often. You can't get a bike by that—unless the tide's way out."

"But," Jerry went on, "we can take a right across from the water tower. There's a dirt road nearer the ocean. It's the one Izzie lives on. I need to check in with her anyway."

"Which house?" Phil called as they made the turn. "It was almost dark when we came by yesterday."

"The small yellow one with the red roof. It's called *High Tide*. Follow me." Jerry stood up on his pedals and took the lead.

Shortly, he pulled in by a garbage can in a wooden rack, and Phil followed. "As you can tell," Jerry said, "these are the backs of the houses along here. The fronts

3

face the ocean." He worked his kickstand into position. "I'll see if Izzie's up yet. I just have to let her know I'm *still kicking*, as she says. Be right back."

Beyond the houses Phil could see shorebirds scissoring above the ocean. Each roar of crashing waves drowned their raucous chatter.

True to his word, Jerry had barely disappeared up the high steps until he was back again. Behind him Izzie waved down to Phil. She wore a purple jump suit, and her straight blond hair was caught up in a ponytail. It was funny how he hardly noticed her last evening when they had come by to pick up Jerry and Sarah to spend the night with them at the campground. Jerry was right. She looked more like an *Izzie* than a grandmother.

"Have fun!" she called out.

"She lives by herself?" Phil asked.

"Yeah, she and my grandad are divorced. But she's got lots of friends. They play bridge all the time."

"Well," Jerry said when they were on their way again, "I'll tell you one thing sisters are good for."

"Spill it," pressured Phil.

"They like to write letters. If they hadn't written after you came to Aiken last summer, we would never have seen each other again."

"You're probably right, but do me a favor. Don't tell them that. I don't know about Sarah, but a compliment goes straight to Marcy's head."

"Sure thing. That is, if you'll return the favor."

"What's that?"

"Don't tell anybody about Gabe. At least, not until we find out what the situation is."

"And how are we going to do that?"

"Listen." Jerry stopped pedaling and faced his friend.

4

"I've been coming to Edisto Island all my life. I know every nook and cranny of this place. You know how to solve mysteries. Didn't you find out the secret of that old inn in Aiken?" His bicycle started to wobble. A pained look passed over his face before he started to pedal again. "I waited for you because I need your help."

Jerry's seriousness caught Phil by surprise. "Don't worry," he said. "I'm game."

Jerry slammed his feet down on the sidewalk and stuck out his right hand. "Gimme five!" he yelled.

Phil grinned and slapped it to him.

Chapter 2

"We made a wise decision when we got this screened enclosure for the camper—what with the mosquitoes around here." Mr. Dunlap sat at the picnic table with the four young people. He sipped his coffee and made a satisfying little sound.

Palmettos, spreading oaks, and wax myrtle bushes interlaced with yucca and prickly cactus to make a private world of the Dunlaps' campsite.

Mrs. Dunlap spooned hash browns onto plates around the picnic table. The aroma of country ham permeated the air.

"Jerry is used to grits for breakfast." Phil gave a big grin. "Remember when I ate some at your house last summer? It wasn't bad, even without cream and sugar."

"I'll have to get some from that store across the road and ask Izzie to tell me how to prepare it," Mrs. Dunlap said.

Sarah brushed back her short dark hair. "Oh, that was at our house in Aiken," she said. "Izzie wouldn't know how. She has Pop-tarts and stuff like that for breakfast. She thinks cooking's a waste of time—except maybe boiling the shrimp she gets from Gabe, an old black man who lives on the island."

At the mention of Gabe, Jerry cut a knowing look to Phil. Then for fear he'd been observed, he added, "Yeah, Izzie'd rather play bridge than anything."

Mrs. Dunlap gave a soft laugh. "Sometimes I'm inclined to agree with Izzie about cooking. This group is going to see lots of sandwiches this week. I plan to relax and enjoy the beauty of the island. I love the big old oaks with the moss hanging down and the oleander bushes." She paused before she added, "You know, I still can't believe things worked out so well for you young people. I think it's wonderful you can renew your friendships of last summer."

Jerry let out an "Mmmm" and swallowed a mouthful of hash browns and ham. "Y'all should have heard Sarah scream when Marcy's letter said Mr. Dunlap was coming South again to do research."

"Sarah scream?" Mrs. Dunlap asked in amazement. "I remember a quiet, shy young lady from last summer."

Jerry's face registered surprise. "Sarah quiet? She's got you fooled."

Mr. Dunlap smiled. "I'll have to say neither girl let too much quiet time roll by last night. Think they had too much catching up to do."

"Sounds like we made a good choice in sleeping on the beach, Jerry." Phil took a big bite of sweet roll.

"Yeah. The only problem was the sun blasting our faces this morning." He gave a fake yawn. "We've already been to the other end of the island where the shrimp boats dock."

"Weren't you fellows bothered by mosquitoes?" Mr. Dunlap asked. "I'd think those thick myrtle bushes over the dunes would be prime breeding grounds."

"We got far enough out for the sea breeze to keep them away," Jerry said. "But if you really want to see some giant mosquitoes, you ought to go back to the Indian Mound. You might like that for your research, Mr. Dunlap."

"Actually, my focus this time is on the Sea Islands just after the Civil War. But I'd like very much to see the Indian Mound. Any takers for this morning?"

"Giant mosquitoes?" Marcy squinched up her face.

"There's repellent in the medicine cabinet," her mother said. In an abrupt change she turned to Sarah, then Jerry. "Shouldn't you check with your gran—with Izzie—about going?"

"We stopped by on our way back from Big Bay Creek. She just said not to get in y'all's way."

"Lucky stiffs," Phil said. "Having a grandmother who has a house on the beach."

"When school's not in, we can come down any time we want now that we're older," Sarah explained. "The only thing is we have to entertain ourselves."

"Yeah," Jerry agreed. "Izzie doesn't like having kids around until they start acting like grown-ups."

Mrs. Dunlap laughed. "Oh, you two," she said. "You have a young, stylish-looking grandmother. We all like our peace and quiet. In fact, while you're visiting the Indian Mound, I plan to take a lounge chair out on the beach and soak up the sights and sounds of this fascinating place."

"With a book, no doubt," her husband teased.

"No doubt," she echoed. "I've already got dibs on *Tales of Edisto*, one of the books we picked up at that wonderful little bookstore on the way into the island."

"The lady who wrote that book, Mrs. Graydon, had a

beach house just down the way from Izzie," Jerry said. "She knew her."

"How nice," Mrs. Dunlap said with genuine interest. "I'm really looking forward to learning about the island."

"Gosh, Jerry," Phil said when he could get him away from the others. "I wish you hadn't mentioned the Indian Mound yet. Dad can never turn down an opportunity to find out anything about the past. We need to get to work on that Gabe thing."

"I didn't know he was that gung ho, but don't worry. The trip might be helpful after all." Seeing the girls approaching, he spoke out of the corner of his mouth. "Tell you what I mean later."

Soon they were in the van and headed the short distance up the highway. Marshland bordered both sides of the road.

With a left turn, they were inside the state park grounds.

"They used to have these cabins on the beach where y'all are camping," Jerry said. "But after a hurricane wrecked them, they decided to have the cabins back up here."

With the directions from a ranger, they climbed out and headed down the two-mile walking trail to the Mound. Moss-shrouded limbs of live oaks curved downward like great arms. Fronded palmettos and trunks of tall tough-skinned palms blended with the undergrowth. Rope-like vines twined around pines and hung in swinging loops. Near their feet sounds of woods life rustled.

"Do you still make bird calls, Jerry?" Marcy asked.

"Yeah, but the shorebirds at Edisto squawk all the time. They don't wait to answer calls."

"You're right about one thing, Jerry." Phil fanned the air about his head with both hands. "These mosquitoes are murder."

"Your mother told us to get the repellent." Mr. Dunlap scolded himself.

"The only thing to do is run," Jerry said. "That creates enough of a breeze to swish them away."

Willing to give his suggestion a try, they all struck out. In moments sounds of heavy breathing filled the narrow pathway. Finally, sweating in the hot, sticky air, they reached the Mound. A great hill of earth and broken shells jutted upward at the edge of a salt tidal creek. Craggy trees and underbrush hugged the sloping earth. At first they all stood panting and taking in the view.

Jerry broke the silence. "The Edistow Indians lived here. That's where the island got its name. Some English earl bought it and gave it as a land grant."

"I hope he paid more for it than they did for New York," Marcy said. "It was sold for trinkets worth about twenty-four dollars."

"Sounds like the same deal," Jerry said. "Some cloth, hatchets, beads, and stuff."

Mr. Dunlap shook his head in distress. "That's one part of our country's history I'm not proud of—the treatment of the American Indian." After a brief silence, he turned to Jerry. "I can't believe I'm fortunate enough to have somebody who knows so much about the local history. You're the answer to my dreams."

"Oh," Jerry said, "there's lots I don't know about the history of Edisto. It's just that I'm interested in Indian things." He surveyed the Mound. "They used to let you dig here. People found arrowheads and old pieces of pottery. Some of them are in the museum. Now they're trying to preserve what's left."

"I'm glad," Mr. Dunlap said. "That's partly what my research is about—preserving history."

They stood quietly for a moment, and Phil wondered if the others felt the presence of the Red Men in the shadowy forest as he did.

When they'd explored over and around the small Mound, Mr. Dunlap said, "Tell you what. I'm going to dash on back to the entrance and talk with the ranger. Whenever you're ready, join me there."

No sooner than he was out of sight, the girls decided to follow. Jerry gave a sigh of relief. "This is just what I was hoping for. Remember I told you Gabe's house is on this creek?"

"You mean this is still Big Bay Creek where we were this morning?"

"Right. And I thought maybe we could spot it from

13

here. I've never seen it, but I've heard it's somewhere on the creek above the marsh line. I'm not even sure there's a road leading to it. Gabe uses his boat all the time."

Standing on a mound made of crushed shells, they strained to look over the twists and turns of the creek. Marshes, some filled with bright green spears of grass, crisscrossed the tidal creek. The briny sea smell was strong.

"The tide's up now," Jerry said. "It's covered the mud flats and oyster beds."

Something splashed at the edge of the water. Phil jumped. "What was that?" he asked.

"Probably a muskrat. All kinds of animals live in these marshes, including rats and possum."

For a brief moment all was as silent as a cemetery. Then Jerry gasped. "Look!" he pointed to a flat-bottom boat at the bend in the creek. Two black men leaned toward each other in conversation. Between them lay a dirty-brown dog.

It's Gabe!" Jerry said in a hoarse whisper.

Chapter 3

Instinctively the boys ducked down behind a yucca bush. Peeking out, they saw Gabe's rowboat rocking gently against the gray-green grass of the tidal marsh. The men's voices carried across the water.

"Huccome oonuh bring me heah?"

"T'ing' ent gwi' right," Gabe answered. "Uh 'peelin' fuh yo hep."

"Wuh de madduh?"

"Two strange buckruh attuh me."

"Wuh dey wonts?"

"Dey wonts me tuh tell'um weh sump'n' at."

"Cyan' oonuh do dat?"

"Melia wunt leh me."

"Oonuh wonts me tuh conjuh 'um. Enty?"

Phil pulled at Jerry's arm. "What are they saying? They sound like ducks quacking."

Jerry put his finger to his lips and strained to pick up the next words.

"Dat right."

"Den git me sump'n' dere's."

"Cyan' do dat. Dunno weh dey be."

"Tawk ent hep."

Without another word, Gabe lifted the oar and gave a shove against the roots of the marsh grass. With the movement, two great white birds erupted behind them, spread their wings, and skimmed over the winding creek.

"What in tarnation was that all about?" Phil's mouth hung open. "It sounded like a foreign language."

"It was Gullah, or partly. You ought to hear some of the people on James Island. You can't pick up on a thing they say. Gabe's a lot easier to understand."

"But what did they say?"

"Gabe was asking the other man to put a spell on the people who are after him. The man told him he'd need something that belonged to them—you know, clothes— to do it. But Gabe said he couldn't get anything, so the man says he can't help him."

"Good grief!" Phil threw his hands up in the air. "I didn't know we were getting tangled up in something like that. And what's *buckruh* anyway?"

"That's what the older blacks call white people, especially the ones they don't like." Jerry leaned to pass under a low-hanging limb. "Now you see what I mean. Gabe needs help, and we gotta help him."

Phil whipped around and faced Jerry accusingly. "Oh, for crying out loud! Don't tell me you believe in that hocus-pocus—that sticking pins in dolls that look like the people and all that junk."

"I didn't say I believed in it. But I'll tell you one thing. If we're going to help Gabe, we have to put ourselves in his place. If he has faith in that conjuring stuff, then we gotta respect that."

"I . . . I don't know—."

"Listen, Phil. The other Sunday a missionary doctor came to our church. He told us the African people wouldn't believe his medicine would cure them. And they didn't get well the way they should have. But, when the missionaries let a witch doctor set up a tent next to their office so the sick people could go by there on the way home—." He stopped to catch his breath. "So he could rattle his gourd over them or whatever he does, they started grinning and getting well."

"Okay. Okay." Phil swatted a mosquito and started walking. "You've brainwashed me. What now?"

"Well, the first thing we gotta do is find out who's following Gabe."

"That sounds reasonable. What then?"

"We get something that belongs to them for the conjurer."

"Now wait a minute, Jerry. If we go stealing something, the police are going to get involved whether we want them to or not."

"We're not going to *steal*; we're going to borrow. You can just imagine how impossible it would be for Gabe to do that."

"Well, we have to find the guilty people first. And, we better be making plans before we get back around those girls."

"You think we ought to let them in on it?" Jerry asked. "Marcy was with you when you solved that mystery in Aiken."

"But she nearly drove me wild to tell Dad. Anyway, I didn't know you that well then. Two's enough—for now anyway."

"Deal," Jerry agreed. "Late this afternoon we can ride our bikes back down to Bay Creek. That's when Gabe fishes—then and early morning. I think he's scared to fish up the creek by himself since those people are after him.

19

He'll probably be around the mouth across from those boat slips. His boat's too small to get out in the Atlantic."

. . . . .

With the first step of their detective work laid out, Phil and Jerry met the others at the park entrance with sealed lips.

"The ranger tells me the museum is just down the road from here," Mr. Dunlap said as they loaded up. "I suggest we give that a spin."

Phil and Jerry exchanged satisfying looks. After all, they wouldn't be able to find Gabe until late afternoon.

"Jerry's been there, but I haven't," Sarah said. "It hasn't been open very long."

"So," Mr. Dunlap said, "it's agreeable then." He made a left turn onto the highway.

"We won't stay long, will we, Dad?" Marcy asked. "We've hardly been on the beach."

"Nope, but midday is no time for the fair-skinned Dunlap tribe to be in the sun."

"I know," Marcy complained, and she and Phil set up a mocking chorus of "We get more freckles; we blister."

Everybody laughed.

"And it's all my fault," her father said. "You kids got my complexion rather than your mom's. Too bad I don't have that nice olive skin like Jerry and Sarah."

Moans surfaced before Mr. Dunlap consoled, "You'll survive. I have."

Along the stretches of marshland, oleanders, and moss-ladened oaks, Jerry pointed out several historical churches. "That Presbyterian graveyard has three missionary teachers from the North buried in it. They were on Edisto teaching the black people who were freed in the War Between the States. They drowned on one of the creeks on Christmas Day. Izzie has a diary one of their friends wrote, and she tells about it."

"Now that figures into my period of research, Jerry. I'm glad you told me. I want to come back to all the churches along here when there's more time. All of them played important parts in the Civil War—or I believe you Southerners prefer to call it the War Between the States." He flashed a smile.

"My social studies teachers made us call it the War of Northern Aggression." Sarah giggled. "She counted off if we didn't."

"Well, whatever," Mr. Dunlap said. "We are all friends now. 'One nation,' as the pledge to the flag says. . . . And here we are."

As they walked toward the museum, Phil decided it would have to be pretty awesome to overpower the thoughts of the investigation they had undertaken. In spite of agreeing to Jerry's proposal, he wasn't at all sold on the idea. What if they got caught stealing clothing from these people? What if Gabe's pursuers turned out to be gangsters? What if they tried to kill the old man and the two of them got in the way? *What-if's* hung on like the gray moss in the surrounding trees as he stepped into the museum.

Chapter 4

The group stood before the exhibit telling the early history of Edisto island.

"Look," Phil said. "This is about that earl from England who bought Edisto from the Indians—the one Jerry was telling us about."

His father, still engrossed in the Indian display, called ahead. "Wait a minute, Son. You're getting the cart before the horse. It says here the Spanish settlers came before the English, and they called the island *Oristo*."

"You know that new development up near where the shrimp boats come in?" Jerry asked. "They named it Oristo after the first settlers."

"Interesting," Mr. Dunlap commented. "Very interesting." And in the next breath, he said, "Okay, Phil, I'm ready for the Earl of Shaftsbury. It says he bought Edisto in 1674."

"And don't miss this," Jerry said from the other side of the narrow room. "I like the way the Colonial people made tabby for the foundations of their houses. See, they burned seashells to make lime. Then they mixed that with water to make something like concrete. You can still see tabby at some of the plantation homes."

They moved on through the small rooms, looking at displays about times when indigo and Carolina Gold rice were grown on the island. They studied weapons of the War Between the States, artifacts, treasures, and letters from the past. Pictures, charts, and maps of the way things used to be lined the walls.

"Sarah," Marcy called. "Look at the waist on this dress. Can you believe it belonged to a lady? Her waist was tinier than mine."

"Ugh!" Sarah sighed. "Just thinking about wearing those high collars and long sleeves and all those petti-coats underneath that long skirt gives me claustrophobia. I'll settle for my shorts and T-shirt any day."

"And look at these high-topped button-up shoes so nobody could see their ankles." Marcy laughed. "They'd really be spaced out if they could come back and see how we dress."

"Wait'll you see the wildlife room." Jerry led the way past the curator's desk and into the room where animals of the area and wildlife had been preserved. "There's one of those big sea turtles that come up on shore this time of year to lay their eggs."

They were still studying the displays of sea animals when Mr. Dunlap joined them. "Hey," he said, noticing how intently Marcy studied the exhibit on turtles. "Who was that rearing to go back to the campsite and the beach?" He put his hand on his daughter's shoulder.

"Look at this loggerhead turtle, Dad," Marcy said.

"Amazing creatures, aren't they?" he responded.

"Izzie helps with the turtle watch." Sarah came up behind them. "She puts little flags along the dunes where a turtle has made a nest and laid eggs."

"That's great," Mr. Dunlap said. "We need to protect our endangered species."

. . . . .

With the thought of getting on the beach pulling at them, they were soon on their way back to the campground.

"Edisto's the very best beach anywhere for finding shells," Sarah said.

"And sharks' teeth," Jerry added. "But if you want to find humongous conchs, you need to go to Botany Bay Island."

"Is it far?" Phil questioned.

"Not really, but if you don't have a boat of your own, you have to ride in a car up to Mead's Boat Landing. Then, you pay a man there to take you across Frampton's Inlet to Botany Bay."

"He leaves you," Sarah said, "and comes back for you whenever you tell him to." She gave a shiver and hugged herself. "One time when Mom and Dad were down, we went. It was cloudy, and there were hardly any other people there. It was weird and kind of scary."

"Awh, not really scary," her brother said. "But it is a barren-looking place with a lot of big pieces of driftwood with Dracula shapes."

"Well, JER—RY," Sarah emphasized his name, "that's just what I was saying."

"I guess the worse part is that once you're on the island and that boat's gone, you know you couldn't get off if it didn't come back for you."

"Couldn't you swim?" Phil asked.

"Swimming around these inlets can be really dangerous, even if you're a good swimmer. Tides get real strong around the barrier island, especially when the tide's going out. The undertow can be tricky too."

"Sounds as if you definitely wouldn't want to swim your way back from Botany Bay Island," Mr. Dunlap said.

Shortly they turned into the campground and wound through the palms, palmettos, and clumps of myrtles until Mr. Dunlap pulled up at the edge of their campsite.

Much to their pleasure, Mrs. Dunlap had ham sandwiches, chips, and frosty canned drinks waiting for a quick lunch.

Afterwards Jerry and Phil agreed it was too early to look for Gabe. They joined the girls on their way to the beach. The short walk took them over their own private path. Mounds of wax myrtle intertwined with fronded palmettos lined each side of the path in a border taller than their heads. Then, like being catapulted into another world, they became engulfed by the smells and sounds of the ocean.

Once accustomed to the sunlight bouncing off white sand, they stopped to take in the view. Out on the horizon shrimp boats bobbed. As far as they could see on their left, the beach stretched endlessly. Here and there jetties of gray rock jutted up into the lapping water. Crushed shells banked against rocks and sea oats hugged sand dunes.

In the other direction a gray pavilion towered against

a blue sky. Big birds rose majestically from the dock pilings and flapped in slow motion. Then, like an airplane about to touch ground, they brought their legs forward and landed without a splash on the water.

Down a way, a dog raced after a receding wave, barking furiously. When a wave rushed toward him, he reeled back and plunged off with a scatter of sand. They all laughed.

"I wish I could have brought Shep," Jerry said."But he's too hard to keep up with down here, and Izzie doesn't like him dripping sandy sea water all over her house."

Sarah and Marcy stood mesmerized by a brown cloud of little birds with matchstick legs. They watched them run along a sand bar, then—all together—change abruptly to scurry in the direction of a shallow tidal pool.

Couples and families milled along the water's edge. Some carried plastic bags for collecting shells. Mothers sat in low-slung chairs watching young children run back and forth as the waves chased them in. The rushing sound of waves swallowed up happy voices.

Nearby, Phil asked, "Don't you go in the ocean?"

"Yeah," Jerry answered, "but you gotta watch out for shells cutting your feet." He hunched over and let his arms dangle. "I like to look for sharks' teeth. Last summer I found zillions of them. I even won a contest sponsored by a real estate company." He straightened up and laughed. "Of course, I didn't have anything else to do— not like we do now anyway." He looked around to make sure their sisters couldn't hear him before he said, "Hey, why don't we go ahead and start scouting around for suspicious-looking people—at least until it's time to find Gabe at the dock."

"Scout where?" Phil asked.

"Mainly around the beach area and the dock. But we could start by hanging around the IGA grocery store. Sooner or later everybody on the island comes in there."

"But how do you know who we're looking for?"

"Oh, you can tell the island people from the tourists. If we see some people who don't look like they *fit in*, we can tell."

Phil looked doubtful. "Well—okay. If you say so. Maybe you can tell who belongs on the island. I doubt I could." He started toward a rise in the beach where Marcy and Sarah bent over a mound of shells. "Let's tell the girls so they can let Mom know."

"Wait a second." Jerry put out his hand to stop Phil. "Let's slip up behind them and see what they're talking about."

"Did you see that couple that just walked by?" Marcy was asking. "She makes two of him."

"They must not be campers," Sarah said. "Not dressed like that. Look at her glitzy top and red stirrup pants. And he's got on cowboy boots."

Marcy giggled. "She looks like a woman wrestler, and he looks like a wimp."

"Is that hair on her head or straw from a packing crate?"

"It's her hair all right," Marcy answered. "The bottom's grown-out bleached junk. The top part's black."

"Well, well—" Phil's voice made them jump from fright. "Just listen to these little sisters of ours. Have you ever considered that couple might not like the way you two look either?"

Marcy's temper flared. "Scram! or I'm telling Mom." She scooped up a handful of crushed shells and threw them at him.

"It's rude to eavesdrop," Sarah burst out. "Anyway, my English teacher said writers are *people watchers,* and we aren't like our dumb brothers. We like to write."

"Jerry—" Phil turned to his friend with a sweep of his arm. "Let me introduce you to the Brontë sisters."

"I mean it, Phil—" Marcy grit her teeth and glared up at him. "You can't boss me around the way you used to."

"Okay. Okay. Calm down. Just tell Mom we're riding our bikes."

"Brothers!" Sarah and Marcy said in unison and turned again to their search for special shells. Each unbroken one excited them.

"Just think how long this shell whirled about in the ocean before it was cast up on the shore," Sarah said in a dreamy mood.

"Yeah. I guess each one could tell its own story if shells could talk."

Soon they were lost in their shell collecting. Even when they looked up the beach to see the strange couple turning up into one of the myrtle-bound paths to a camp-site, it no longer interested them.

Chapter 5

Phil and Jerry propped their bikes outside the island grocery.

"Let's be doing something so we won't look suspicious," Phil said.

"What do you suggest?" Jerry looked around. A machine for ice. A rack for empty drink bottles. Some newspaper racks. "No kids are going to stand around reading newspaper headlines," he said. "That'd really draw attention to us."

A van filled with fussing children pulled up. The mother got out and leaned to unbuckle the youngest from his car seat. Swinging him to her hip, she went into the store. Inside the van the others screeched and yelled. "I'm telling!" a girl whined.

A jacked-up pickup sped into the parking lot and jerked to a stop. Two house painters—their coveralls splotched with white paint—climbed out. Jerry cupped his hand around his mouth and leaned toward Phil. "You think they might be using that paint business as a disguise? Criminals do that, you know—try to look like they're somebody they're not."

Phil tiptoed to look in the bed of the truck. "They've

got paint cans back here. And they've been used. A ladder too."

A blue Honda with two ladies drove up. Jerry recognized them as Izzie's bridge partners.

"Hello there, Jerry," one said in a cheery voice. "This must be your New York friend Izzie told us about."

"Yes, Ma'am," Jerry said. "This is Phil Dunlap. He's staying at the campground. His father researches history."

"That's what we hear." She brought her eyebrows together in a way that dropped her glasses down on her nose. "*But the campground?* That sounds SO uncomfortable. Do tell them about the Trudies' house, Jerry. It's available for rent this week."

"We like camping," Phil heard himself say.

"Yeah. So do I," Jerry added. "We slept on the dunes last night."

"Oh, my." It was the other lady's turn to squinch up her nose. "Things could crawl on you, you know."

"We need to hurry, Maisie," her friend said. "We're holding up the bridge game." She fluttered her hand in a goodbye. "We'll tell Izzie we saw you."

"Come on, Phil. This is not working out." Jerry hopped on his bike. "Let's ride on down to the dock where we were yesterday. Maybe Gabe's already there. If we can get him to tell us what the people look like who are after him, at least we'll know who we're looking for."

"I sure go along with that. We're not getting anywhere like this."

They rode lazily down Palmetto Boulevard, picking up sounds from houses they passed and watching out for scattered traffic.

"Looks like solving this mystery is going to be tougher

than you thought," Phil offered halfheartedly.

"It's just that we gotta have Gabe's cooperation. That's the bottom line, as they say."

"Yeah. And we need to find out *why* somebody would be after him."

"We will," Jerry assured his friend. "We just have to take it easy so we won't scare him off."

Around the bend they passed Oristo's golf course and the new gray houses and condominiums on the left. On the creek, gulls swooped and shrieked over docked shrimp boats.

Even before they got close enough to park their bikes, the fishy smell of the day's catch engulfed them. Voices called back and forth as crews cleaned boats.

"Look," Jerry said. "There's the man who ran Gabe off his shrimp boat yesterday morning."

"*Sea Pride*," Phil read. "That's the name of his boat."

Jerry caught his breath. "And there's Gabe."

Down a way the old man sat on a low bench with his back against a shed. He bent over a shrimp net—spread out around him—with a long kind of needle hook. His dog slept at his feet.

"Come on," Jerry said and started toward him.

Phil opened his mouth to ask "What will you say to him? He'll know we eavesdropped on him and the other man at the Indian Mound." But he was too late. Jerry was already greeting Gabe. To Phil's surprise, the dog did not even raise his head.

"Remember me?" Jerry was saying. "You always bring my grandmother fish down at High Tide, but we haven't seen you lately. Are the fish not biting?"

Without looking up, Gabe mumbled, "Ent fish much letly."

"What's your dog's name?" Phil asked.

"'E name Eben. " Gabe still did not look up from the tangle of cords.

"*Eben?*" Phil repeated. It didn't sound like any dog's name he'd ever heard before. He gave Jerry a quizzical look.

"Uh calls 'im Dawg mosely. But 'e name Eben 'kase 'e

eben tempuh. 'E don' nebbuh mek no fuss 'bout nutt'n'."

Jerry and Phil exchanged smiles.

"Gabe," Jerry said in a friendly manner, "I'll bet Izzie—that's my grandmother—would like you to bring her some shrimp. My friend here and his family are visiting from up North."

"Uh sho try." For a moment he seemed in deep thought. "Mebbe kin tek de shawtcut 'fo' dayclean."

Phil gave Jerry a questioning look and heard him ask, "Why would you have to fish before daybreak?"

Gabe looked up at them. His eyes had a yellow cast with lids that seemed paper thin. He took a long shivery breath and laid down the net. Without moving his head, he rolled his eyes in every direction. Then in a low voice he said, "Hit disaway. Two buckruh—stranjuh tuh de islant—attuh me." He put his hand up to his forehead and stroked it with long slender fingers. "One way nurrah, dey gone git me."

Jerry stooped down in front of him. "We want to help you, Gabe. You can trust us. My friend Phil is good at helping people. He took care of an old man and his wife last summer, and—"

Jerry looked up at Phil and back at Gabe, took a quick breath, and continued in a low, slow voice. "What do these people who are after you look like?"

For a moment Gabe looked as if he was in a stupor. Then he held up his slender arms to make a halo around his head. "Hit uh big 'ooman wid uh head uh hair. En' uh leetle biddy shawt man."

A flash shot through Phil and Jerry at the same time. THE COUPLE ON THE BEACH THAT MARCY AND SARAH WERE DESCRIBING!

"Does the woman have straw hair?" Phil blurted out

almost too loudly.

"And does the man wear cowboy boots?" Jerry fired.

"Dey duz. Dey sho duz."

"Gabe," Jerry's voice was serious. "We have to tell you something." He glanced at Phil and received a go-ahead. "We were at the Indian Mound yesterday, and we heard you talking to the conjure man."

"Oonuh heah me?" Gabe jerked back, his face registering shock.

"It's all right, Gabe." Phil stooped down and put his hand on the old man's knee.

"Yeah," Jerry said. "Everything's going to be all right. We had to tell you because we're going to get some possessions—some clothes—that belong to these people for you to give to the conjure man." His voice lost some wind as he added, "As soon as we find out where they are staying on the island."

"T'ank de Lawd," Gabe said, his face brightening. "T'ank de Lawd. Uh be 'roun' dese sheds en' de crick. Figguh dey ent gone bodduh me 'roun' odduh foke." He shook his head. "Cyan' go home. Dey dun been dere."

"We'll be back as soon as we can," Jerry promised.

"Dat good." Gabe nooded. "Dat good."

They left him still nodding his head like a bobber nibbled by a fish. Even after he picked his net back up, he was still nodding.

Eager to get away from the dock so they could discuss their meeting with Gabe, they pedaled fast.

Out of earshot, Phil turned to Jerry. "Why didn't you ask him who Melia was while you had him talking?"

"I thought maybe we shouldn't push him too far. You could see how upset he got when he found out we heard him at the Indian Mound. But the way I figure it, that conjure man knows who Melia is."

"How do you figure that?"

"Because when Gabe told him Melia wouldn't let him tell the buckruh what they wanted to know, the man settled for that. That's when he told him to get something of theirs—for the spell—and bring to him."

"Is that how the conversation ended?"

"Not quite. Gabe said he couldn't get anything because he didn't know where to find them. But, of course, we know he couldn't anyway. They'd probably shoot him if he tried. That's why we have to do it for him."

"Okay. That makes sense. I just wanted to be sure I had all the facts straight. We can't afford to be too careful. So they just left things kind of hanging?"

"Yep. The man told Gabe talking wasn't going to do any good—meaning he needed possessions to put the spell on. I guess Gabe didn't see any need to argue with him about that."

For the rest of the way to the campground, each felt the other was lost in the same thoughts—thoughts about a woman with weird hair and a skinny man in Western clothes.

Just who was this couple? Where could they find them? And if they did find them, how would they manage to get some of their clothing? Who was Melia? And most importantly, what was the question Gabe couldn't answer?

Chapter 6

"Well," Phil said as they neared the campground, "first things first, as they say."

"Find the couple?"

"Right. And I've been wondering. Do you think the girls may have seen them again on the beach?"

"They had to walk back by them. There are no houses up toward Jeremy Creek, and that's the way they were headed."

"But, if the girls are still sore at us for teasing them, they won't tell even if they did see them. At least Marcy won't. She's bad to hold a grudge."

"Come on," Jerry urged. "Let's give it a try. We don't have anything to lose."

The activity at the Dunlaps' campsite told them that pumping their sisters for information would have to be put on hold—at least for the time being.

Mr. Dunlap was grilling hamburgers under a sprawling oak. "Perfect timing!" he called. "These burgers are right ready to come off the grill."

"They smell great," Phil said, coming up close to the sizzling patties. He breathed in the meaty smell of the swirling smoke.

"I'll say," Jerry agreed.

Marcy and Sarah worked at ignoring their brothers as they brought out the condiments, silverware, and napkins. At a table against the camper, they filled paper cups from ice in a cooler. Mrs. Dunlap held pot holders around a steaming dish of baked beans. "Wash up, fellows," she said. "Soup's on."

During the meal, Mr. Dunlap—as usual—got caught up in telling them things he had already learned about Edisto Island. "Did anybody know salt was manufactured off Botany Bay?" he questioned. "They used the creeks as evaporating ponds. Of course that was before the period I'm researching, but I enjoy reading about other time periods as well."

"I didn't know about the salt," Jerry said, "but what time period are you researching, Mr. Dunlap?"

"Just after the Civil War when *our* infamous General William Tecumsah Sherman made his march across South Carolina."

"Yeah," Jerry blurted out, forgetting the food in his mouth. "He did that to punish us for being the first state to secede from the Union."

"Oh?" Mr. Dunlap hurried on. "Maybe you Southerners know that ten thousand freed blacks followed Sherman's soldiers in their march to the sea. Can you imagine? *Ten thousand homeless people on these sea islands.* I'm interested in finding out how everyone coped with that situation and what happened to all those people."

"Honey," his wife urged, "don't forget to eat."

At the word "homeless," Phil glanced at Jerry. Was he wondering too where Gabe would sleep tonight?

Mr. Dunlap took a healthy bite of his burger, chewed, and swallowed. "Let me back up a bit," he said, reminding Sarah of her social studies teacher. "The Southern general who was in charge of defending the Low Country against the *Yanks*—"

"Yeah—" Jerry interrupted. "THOSE DAMN YAN-KEES!" He was really getting into it now.

"Hold on—" Mr. Dunlap laughed and waved him down. "Years before the march, that general ordered the islands evacuated because it was impossible to defend them."

"Union forces had gunboats all up these creeks," Jerry said. "Nobody could withstand that."

"True." Mr. Dunlap tackled his food again.

"I've been reading about some of the plantation homes." Mrs. Dunlap's voice had a calming effect. "It's so sad the planters and their families had to leave their fine furniture when they evacuated. Much of it had come on ships from abroad: great mirrors in gold-lead frames, banquet-sized tables, damask draperies. And libraries filled with beautiful leather-bound books. Not to speak of all the silver: coffee and tea service sets, bowls, goblets, flat-ware."

"We studied in school," Sarah said, "that the planta-tion owners buried their silver before they left so the soldiers wouldn't carry it off."

"Where did the planters' families go?" Marcy asked.

"To the Up Country of South Carolina," Jerry spoke up, "to stay with relatives—at least the women and chil-dren did. The men were away fighting."

"Why didn't they take their things with them?" Marcy asked.

"Remember," her father said. "This is in time of war. Besides, they are on an island that has no bridge to the mainland. Work horses have been given to the war effort.

All able-bodied men are gone. I understand that at this time the sea islands became a *no-man's land* with plundering and vandalism."

"The Union soldiers even took the pipe organ out of the Presbyterian Church and shipped it up North." Jerry twisted his mouth in a joking way before he said, "You *Yanks* really were bad."

"You're right," Mr. Dunlap said. "People on both sides do terrible things in war times. There's pillaging and destruction—things those same people wouldn't dream of doing in peace time."

Phil shifted on the picnic bench. He'd have to admit this was more interesting than any history his father had gotten into yet, but it was going to be dark soon. He and Jerry had plans. "What's for dessert?" he asked.

"IGA cookie special." His mother smiled. "You can get the package from the kitchen."

When Phil returned with the cookies, his father was going stronger than ever. "Then, of course, Union soldiers lived in the planters' homes."

"What happened to the poor homeless persons who followed the soldiers?" his wife asked.

"That was the real problem. Military authorities had failed to make sufficient plans for them. Many had become ill; all were hungry. They, too, were allowed to live in the vacated homes, though space was inadequate. Fortunately, a Freedmen's Bureau organized in New England came to their rescue. They sent food, clothing, and even teachers to the islands.

"And three of the teachers drowned on one of the creeks," Jerry said. "I told you about that when we passed the Presbyterian Church where they're buried. Remember?"

Phil stood up. "It's going to be dark soon."

"You're right." His mother looked at Marcy. "If you're spending the night with Sarah, you'll need to be getting off—that is, if you're walking."

"Could I just wind up this part by saying the planters—some of them anyway—did eventually move back into their homes." Although Mr. Dunlap had seemed to make a request, he really didn't expect an answer. "It must have been a nightmare for those who returned from the War to find their homes taken over, their cattle and possessions carried off, their Confederate money worthless. At any rate, General Howard, who headed up the Freedmen's Bureau, told the freedmen and their teachers they must give up the homes, churches, and land taken over during the War."

"So, what on earth did all these displaced persons do?" his wife asked.

"Some left for Charleston where they hoped the Bureau would care for them. Most stayed. Some worked for the planters and were allowed to buy land. Others were given land taken over by the government for unpaid taxes. Many of them built little places along the creek, and they've been here ever since."

"Gabe, the old fisherman I told you about, lives in a little house up on the creek," Sarah said. "I'll bet his family got their land that way."

At the mention of Gabe, Phil jerked to attention and dared to look at Jerry. His lips were down tight.

"That would probably be his grandparents who received the small land grant," Mr. Dunlap surmised.

Mrs. Dunlap began to gather up plates. "I know I've heard some of this before, but I guess it didn't stick. There's nothing like being on the spot where history was made."

Her husband leaned over and gave her a hug. "That's why I married this woman," he said.

"Mom," Phil said, "since it's getting dark, Jerry and I can walk the girls up to Izzie's."

"How sweet of you to think of it, Phil."

He turned away quickly. He didn't want to see the pleased look she'd be giving him. He felt guilty enough already.

. . . . .

"Okay, Phil, come clean," Marcy said as soon as they were over the myrtle-enclosed path and on the beach. "Why are you being so nice to us?"

"Nice? Me? Do I look like the nice-guy type?"

"You not only don't look like the nice-guy type," Marcy shot back, "most of the time you don't act like one either."

Phil dropped back a couple of steps and motioned to Jerry. "You ask them about the couple," he whispered. "They don't trust me."

Jerry scratched his head and hesitated before he asked, "Ah . . . by the way, did you . . . ah . . . two *writers* get an opportunity to *observe* that funny-looking couple again on the beach?"

"Why do you two want to know?" Sarah questioned.

"We're just curious," Jerry replied.

"Oh?" Marcy spoke up. "Since when did boys have that trait? I thought only cats and girls were curious."

"Funny, Marcy. Very funny," Phil remarked.

Marcy giggled. She was having a better time on this trip than she ever imagined. "Look how the moon makes a silver path across the ocean," she said.

"I love the sea," Sarah said dreamily, "except when it's stormy."

"Well, Jerry—" Phil spoke louder and slower than usual so their sisters would be sure to hear him. "There's your grandmother's house. We can go on back now. I guess Sarah and Marcy didn't see that couple again, or they would have told us."

The girls exchanged glances, giggled, and ran toward the dune leading to Izzie's steps.

"Dang!" Phil said, "They make me mad."

"Me too," Jerry agreed.

They had turned and started back down the beach when Marcy called out from the deck of High Tide. "Hey, Phil, in case you're still interested, we saw them go up one of those paths at the far end of the campground."

Chapter 7

Phil and Jerry stood like robots and stared blankly at each other. Then Phil gave a low whistle through his teeth. "Did I hear what I thought I heard?"

"You heard it right. That couple is at the campground. I can't believe it either. They definitely didn't look like campers."

Jerry motioned a 'Come on' and started down the beach. "The campground's lighted. Maybe we can spot them."

"What if we do?"

"Then we'll try to get something that belongs to them for Gabe to give his conjure friend." He jumped sideways to avoid the tide rushing in on curling foam.

Phil put his hand up to his head in thought. "Trying to get a possession is going to be a *real* problem. Maybe we should go to the police after all, Jerry, or at least tell—"

"Phil—" Jerry stopped and faced his friend. "Answer me this: did police officers come to your school when you were little and tell you they were your friends?"

"Sure, but what's that got to do with anything?"

"Well, they didn't do that for Gabe. For one thing, most blacks his age never even went to school. They can print their names and make change, and that's about it."

"I still don't see—"

"The fact is that the word POLICE means one thing to most of these old blacks, and that's JAIL."

"But—"

"Trust me, Phil. Gabe won't talk to the police. If we don't help him, something's likely to happen to him. And for somebody that old, the authorities would probably decide he died of natural causes."

They hopped over a trench of water where the sea had furrowed inland. "Where's that path to our campsite anyway?" Phil asked. "They all look alike. We should have brought along a flashlight."

"You're not supposed to use them on the beach this time of year. Izzie helps with the turtle patrol, and she says if eggs are hatching and the babies see a light, they go toward it rather than the moonlight on the water. Then they end up being eaten by a predator or run over by a car on the road. Most people won't burn outside lights on the water side for that reason."

Suddenly Phil felt left out of things. There was so much he didn't know about the island and its people. "You know, Jerry," he said, "you really don't need me to help you at all."

"Are you kidding? It was your idea to ask the girls if they'd seen the couple again. You have good ideas. With what I know about the island, we make a team."

"Well, all right." Phil felt his frustration draining away. "Dr. Watson reporting, Sherlock Holmes."

Even in the gray light of evening, Phil saw his friend flash a big smile.

Jerry pointed ahead. "I think that's our path," he said. "There's a big palmetto log next to it. That'll help us spot it

44

in the future."

At the camper both Dunlaps were reading. With a quick report on the girls delivered, Phil anounced, "Jerry and I are going to walk around the campground."

"Good idea." His mother looked up from her book. "You may meet some other youngsters your age."

They acknowledged the high sign Mr. Dunlap gave with a circle of his thumb and forefinger and were off.

Outside, lights on tall poles shone down with a weak, watery look.

"Let's walk around the road and see if we can pick out their site," Phil said.

"Okay. We look for a woman wrestler with hair like straw and a skinny little man in cowboy boots."

"Yeah. I guess she'd be easier to spot than he would. He may not still be wearing those boots. Besides, we might not be able to see his feet in the dark."

Like the Dunlaps' site, the ones on their right were enclosed in a tangle of myrtle and low palmetto fronds. People laughed and talked in loud voices. "I think you should send that to the newspaper," a female voice said.

On their left, tents and trailers nestled under gnarled oaks with beards of gray moss and stately palms. A baby whimpered, and a dog yipped and scratched on a metal camper door to get out.

Some of the sites were dark except for the dim overhead lights of the campground. Somewhere a trailer door slammed. Suddenly a little humpbacked animal scurried from his hiding place in the brush, shot them a hasty glance from its bandit-looking face, and darted into the thick brush.

"What was that?" Phil asked.

"A raccoon. They come out at night and get into garbage cans."

Again they strained their eyes to find the big woman with funny hair. Once they backed up for another look, but the lady's hair didn't look wild enough, and it didn't have the dark part at the top the way Marcy had described.

"Gosh," Jerry said, "I never knew this place was so big."

"It's big all right. Maybe one of the dark sites is theirs."

They followed the curve of the winding road until they found themselves back near the entrance of the campground with its office building and bathhouse. At the well-lighted area with picnic tables and trash cans, they turned back.

"We didn't go this way," Jerry said. "Let's try this road."

Shortly they passed a group of boys throwing darts at a target on an oak limb. If a player missed the limb entirely, the others *boooed* him.

"If we lose anymore darts," someone shouted, "we won't have enough to play."

"A car!" Jerry yanked at Phil's arm, and they backed up out of the road to let it pass. "Good grief! He could have hit us. He was driving too fast for a campground."

"*He* nothing! Did you see that hair?" Phil started in a jog. "Hurry. Let's see where they're headed."

They rushed along the dirt road, stumbling over dips in the ruts. Except for an occasional barking dog, the two shadows racing after the speeding rattle of a car went unnoticed.

For a second they thought they had lost it. Then ahead, brakes screeched and headlights glanced off trees.

"Th—that car's a . . . piece of junk." Jerry's breath came

in spurts. "I didn't know the camping sites . . . went this far. It looks deserted back here."

"Look," Phil gasped. "They're turning in." He motioned to Jerry, and they eased into a path through the myrtle and made a loop behind the site.

Completely hidden by the thick undergrowth, they peeked through at the scene before them. The car had pulled in by a boat on a trailer. Nothing else was on the campsite. A jumble of camping equipment stuck up from the boat.

In the dimly lit area they saw the small, thin man reach into the boat and tug at something that looked like a tent.

The woman climbed out of the car. "I told you to leave the tent pitched!" she screamed in a coarse voice from the other side of the boat. "You never listen."

"I thought we'd nab the old man and be outa here," he argued. "I told you that a hundred times already."

Mosquitoes whined around Phil and Jerry, but they dared not move.

"And whose dumb idea was it to stake out the old man's house for the last six hours? Tell me that. I shoulda known he wadn't stayin' there after our last *get-together* with him. But NO, I listened to you for once." Her voice lost some of its coarseness and moved to a high nagging tone. "I told you he hangs around that dock where the shrimp boats come in. But I can't tell you anything. From now on, I'm callin' all the shots."

"I guess you think your *know-it-all* Biff could do better."

"At least he's got some smarts."

All the time they fussed, they jerked and pulled at things in the boat, clanging and scraping them together

47

and throwing them out on the ground.

"Just because he sits with them books in his hand all the time, don't mean he's got no common sense. I say we go back to gettin' the stuff the way we been doin'."

"Here we go again," she harped. "For the last time, Biff says this is fine stuff without records on it."

"Well, I don't like it."

"Like it or not, we're finishin' up this job just like Biff told us to. Wadn't for him, we never woulda pulled off that one in Beaufort."

"And how much did you get out of it? Answer me that."

"Don't you worry your simple head about the money," she snapped at him. "But, for your information, the pay-off comes *after* the deal—unless you act stupid again and botch it."

The man didn't answer. Instead, he moved to the passenger side of the car and reached in for something. In moments the boys saw a tiny red glow rise and fall as he drew on a cigarette.

Chapter 8

Like a curtain drawn on a play, the action seemed to be over. Phil and Jerry edged their way out of the myrtle, slipped down far enough not to be detected by the couple, and took the loop back to their campsite. To any onlookers they were just two boys strolling along to kill time.

"Now do you believe it?" Jerry asked, making sure to keep his voice low.

"I never said I didn't believe it." For some reason Phil's legs felt rubbery. "But you have to admit, it all sounds too strange to be true. I mean, it's just like something you see on TV. What *stuff* were they talking about?"

"It's a mystery to me. You wouldn't think Gabe would have anything they'd be interested in."

"Maybe he doesn't actually *have* it. Didn't you say the conjure man wanted Gabe to tell them where something *was*?"

"THAT'S RIGHT! And whatever they're looking for at Edisto is like something they've gotten in Beaufort. That's down the coast from here."

Phil stepped out to dodge a dark spot in the road that looked like a hole. "I'm glad Gabe was smart enough not to go back to his house."

"Me too. They could do anything to him way up that creek, and nobody'd ever hear them."

Phil shook off the shiver running over his back. They were in this situation now, good and deep. "The question is," he said, "how are we ever going to get any possessions? I'll bet they keep their clothes in the car. If that's the case, when they're gone, their clothes will be too."

"Yeah. You're probably right."

"Now, the other thing we need to concentrate on is helping Gabe hide from them. From the way they talked, I don't think they'll be going back out tonight. But they'll be looking for him around the dock tomorrow. And one thing's for sure: they mean business."

"You can say that again."

"Holy mackerel!" Phil scratched at his arms like a mad man. "Something's bitten me all over."

"Mosquitoes. Me too. Those myrtle bushes are full of them unless there's a strong breeze from the ocean." Jerry alternated scratching and rubbing.

"Let's hurry. Mom's got calamine lotion."

By the time they reached the campsite, they had scratched their bites into red bumps. Mrs. Dunlap expressed sympathy as the boys plastered themselves with the chalky substance.

"I was just telling your father about something in Mrs. Graydon's book. It's about that Gullah dialect the older blacks on the islands use." She tilted her head in Jerry's direction. "I'm sure you know what I'm talking about, Jerry."

"Oh, yes Ma'am. Phil does too. We heard two old black men talking that way yesterday."

Phil shot Jerry a quick look.

"I heard it at the store today, and I was fascinated. It

sounds so—so musical. But, quite frankly, I couldn't understand a word of it."

"I'll bet the store owners could," Jerry said.

"You're right. They could. Anyway, as the story goes, during World War II the Japanese were intercepting our code messages. An officer heard one of the Edisto Island blacks speak and decided to train him to broadcast to our armed forces. With a Gullah interpreter on the other end, it worked. To the amazement of the Japanese, no one could decipher the new *code*."

"Neat!" Jerry said.

"You could be an interpreter, Jerry," Phil told his friend. "You're good at figuring it out."

"I can't always," he said, "but knowing some of them use 'oonuh' for 'you' helps."

"You know—" Mr. Dunlap looked up from his reading. "Gullah isn't actually a dialect. It's a language. It came to this country from Angola when slaves were brought over. It's part of our American heritage made by the African-American people."

"Then it should be preserved." Mrs. Dunlap showed genuine concern.

"You're right," her husband said. "And thank goodness efforts are being made to do that. The only problem is that in the beginning it was not a written language."

The Dunlaps returned to their reading. Phil handed Jerry two chilled drinks from the little camper refrigerator, picked up the portable TV and carried it out to the screened enclosure.

"This reception's terrible," Phil called to whoever was listening. He flipped the control around several times. "The stations that come in half-way decent aren't worth watching," he complained.

"Why don't we go on down to the beach," Jerry suggested. "There won't be mosquitoes if we get out from under the trees."

"They couldn't find another spot to suck blood on me." Phil let out a nervous kind of laugh. "I'll take the lotion in case we can't sleep for itching."

"So early?" Mrs. Dunlap asked when she heard their plans.

"There's nothing else to do." Phil pulled at the sleeping bags they'd stored in the bottom of the narrow closet.

"And we might get lucky enough to see a loggerhead come ashore before we bed down," Jerry answered.

"You know," Mrs. Dunlap commented, "last night I was so pooped I didn't even wake up all night to worry about you fellows sleeping down there all by yourselves."

"It's just over the dunes," Phil said. "Right at the other side of the myrtle bushes."

"This beach is the safest place you could be," Jerry assured them all. "The only crime they ever have around here is something stolen now and then. There aren't any kidnappings or murders or anything like that."

Phil felt the shiver he had experienced earlier run over him again. Did Jerry realize what he had just said? There was always a first time for everything. The situation with Gabe could be just that.

"Phil," his mother was looking directly at him. "Are you all right?"

"Ah—oh, yes. I'm okay. That is, as far as I can be with all these stings."

"Salt water would help," Jerry offered.

"Now, wait a minute," Mrs. Dunlap sat up in her chair. "That's when I put my foot down. No swimming at night."

"Oh, I didn't mean swimming, Mrs. Dunlap," Jerry spoke apologetically. "I only meant splashing it up from the edge."

"Well," Mrs. Dunlap sighed, "that might be acceptable."

"You don't have to worry about us and the ocean," Jerry continued. "The tides on this beach are nothing to fool around with. Sarah and I were taught early not to take any chances."

"I'm sure you're very sensible, Jerry." Phil thought his mother sounded like she was telling somebody she was sorry his dog died. "I'm so glad Phil has you for a friend."

With their night gear stored at the edge of the myrtles, the boys walked along the moonlit beach. The roar of the ocean held their voices in the space between them.

"You know, Jerry, I hate to say this because it sounds just like Marcy when we were exploring that old inn in Aiken, but I do feel guilty keeping this thing about Gabe from my parents. Maybe Dad—"

"Phil, answer me this. What's the first thing your dad would do?"

Phil hesitated before he said, "Call the police."

"Right. And if we reported what we've heard and seen, it would be that couples' word against ours. Who's going to believe two kids and an old black man?"

What Jerry was saying did make sense. "Well, I see your point. But I do want Dad to get to interview Gabe. He wants to record some conversations with older blacks on the sea islands."

"He can if we get this thing cleared up. If we don't, Gabe may not be around by the end of the week."

Each deep in his own thoughts, they walked the deserted beach in silence. The smell, taste, and sound of the ocean rushed about them. The night made sea and sky seem to blend together. A thin wisp of a cloud—or was it a band of fog?—floated here and there.

At the sight of the lighted pavilion, they turned and started back. To their left, the tall trees and thick undergrowth hid the campground from view. Only the glow of the dim lights let them know there were people on the other side of the myrtle-covered dunes.

"Jerry!" Phil called out louder than he meant to. "I've got an idea."

"Spill it."

"Why don't we talk the girls into sneaking the possessions?"

"You mean let them in on our plans?"

"They're already on to the fact we're doing something. I could tell by the way Marcy held the information about the couple until the last minute."

"Hmmmm—I hate to admit it, but they could possibly be helpful. And you know, if we should get caught in the act, it would be harder to—to *dispose* of four kids than two."

Was Jerry's voice shaking, or did Phil imagine it? Down a way, Phil recognized the palmetto log marking their spot. He pointed toward it, and they headed in that direction. Tomorrow was going to be a crucial day. Beneath all his mosquito bites, he could feel it in his bones.

Chapter 9

When the boys came up from their sand-dune burrow, they found the girls and Izzie with the Dunlaps on the screened enclosure.

"Well, good morning," Mrs. Dunlap greeted them. "The girls were just telling us about going on the Turtle Watch with Izzie."

"Yeah." Sarah gave a fake yawn. "She got us up at the crack of day."

Izzie laughed. "That's what it's all about." She turned to the tousled-looking boys where they had dropped their sleeping bags and plopped on them. "We have to get to the beach before walkers mess up turtle tracks made during the night. Otherwise, we can't determine where eggs have been laid and stick up those little markers."

"We had to move one nest," explained Marcy. "It wasn't protected enough by the sea oats, and we thought predators might bother the eggs—or the hatchlings—if they were born in that open area."

"The main predators are raccoons and ghost crabs," Sarah added.

"And," Marcy said, "we dug another bottle-shaped hole just like the one the mother dug with her hind

55

flippers."

"We picked up plastic bags left on the beach, too," Sarah added. "You know turtles think they're jelly fish and eat them."

"Often that's fatal," Izzie explained.

Phil looked confused. "You mean turtles feed on jelly fish? Those stinging things?"

"That *is* hard to understand," Izzie answered, "but they do. Just in case any of their tentacles ever get you, I swear by meat tenderizer applied in a hurry."

"How interesting!" Mrs. Dunlap marveled. "I'll remember that."

Sarah took on a sorrowful expression. "I think it's kind of sad. The mamma turtle lays her eggs, and—" She interrupted herself with "How many eggs does she lay, Izzie?"

"Around a hundred."

A "Wow!" came from Phil and his father at the same time.

"Anyway," Sarah continued, "I think it's sad that after she lays her eggs, she turns around and goes back to the sea without ever coming back."

"I don't blame her," Jerry said. "If I thought I'd have a hundred kids, I'd run away too."

"But just think," Sarah said, refusing to smile with the others over Jerry's remark. "Those little babies have to come into the world without a mother to love and care for them."

Jerry shrugged his shoulders. "I'm sure they have big brothers."

Even Sarah laughed at that. "Oh, and that makes them lucky. *Very lucky.*"

"Okay, fellows. I know you're hungry." Mrs. Dunlap

hopped up. "I'll have some French toast for you in a jiffy."

"I'm glad the loggerheads are being protected by the Endangered and Threatened Species Act," Mr. Dunlap said as the boys followed his wife into the camper.

"So am I," Izzie said. "Lighting in beach areas is regulated so hatchlings won't be lured away from the sea. And the ordinance about using turtle excluder devices is good, even though it isn't popular with most shrimpers."

Marcy reached for a bag of shells she and Sarah had collected and spread them out before them. "I wish I could make a shell necklace," she said.

Sarah picked up one and examined it. "The problem is making holes to string them. They crack."

"That's an Angel Wing." Izzie leaned over to point to the soft white half shell in the shape of a bird wing. "It's my favorite."

"I like the Kitten Paw." Sarah held up a tiny shell with brown ridges. "See. Doesn't it look like a kitten's foot?"

By the time Jerry and Phil rejoined the group, the conversation had turned to history, as it usually did with Mr. Dunlap around. "I'm sort of getting information piecemeal about this Edingsville Beach that is no more," he was saying to Izzie. "All traces of civilization were really washed away?"

"That's right. In the hurricane of 1893. Everything not already devastated by the War Between the States was destroyed. In fact, the force of the winds almost swept the island itself into the sea. All that remains today is a sandbar."

Izzie smiled and leaned back in her chair in a dreamy way. "From all accounts, Edingsville was a paradise. Around fifty wealthy planters and their families went there in summers. The large homes were always filled with guests. Each day wagons brought fresh vegetables. Cows, led over the causeway, provided fresh milk for the children."

"It does sound like a paradise," agreed Mr. Dunlap.

"Ah, yes," Izzie said. "Planters in the Low Country referred to it as the *Riviera*." She looked at her watch and jumped up like a Jack-in-the-Box. "Oh, dear. I've got to hurry. Bridge starts early today. Coming with me, girls?"

"We plan to build a giant sand castle," her granddaughter said.

Phil looked at Jerry. Silently they communicated. They could talk to the girls on the beach about getting the clothing for Gabe.

"First," Phil said when they were alone, "we need to ride to the dock and check on Gabe. It'll take the girls all morning to make a castle."

"Yeah," Jerry agreed. "I just hope those people haven't gotten to him."

Alternating standing and sitting on their bikes, they pedaled toward the dock. Life moved slowly in the small island town. Now and then a car pulled out of a side road and headed toward the main highway leading off the island. Colorful beach towels hung over deck rails on their right. Soon sun worshippers and playful children would be taking them down to the beach to soak up the sights, sounds, and sun.

Nearer the dock, a delivery truck backed up to a restaurant. Across the way, bright shirts of early-morning golfers moved over the greens.

Things were quiet at Bay Creek Marina. Shrimp boats had already gone for the day. They parked their bikes by the high fence separating the condos from the dock area and headed toward the creek.

"Hey," Jerry said, "that's Gabe's *Trus-me-Gawd*."

"His *what*?"

"His boat. That's what the older blacks call their row boats. It means I trust my God. And let me tell you, they need to if they get out on the ocean in those things."

They moved around a shed, obviously a maintenance shop for boats. The garage-type door was up, and they could see all kinds of big machinery inside. Down a way was the building where they had found Gabe mending his shrimp net. No action there either. Only the rowdy cry of shorebirds broke the silence.

Suddenly Jerry made a gurgle of a sound as if he choked on his words and pointed toward the road. The rattletrap of a car they had seen at the campground last night was leaving the paved road and heading up the narrow dirt entrance to the dock area. In the light of day the car was a putrid green, and it headed straight toward them.

59

Chapter 10

"Run!" Phil yelled. For all they were worth, they dashed to the maintenance shed. Inside, they scrunched down behind a big piece of machinery. Breathing heavily, they gulped in the smells of rust and oil. Outside, creaks and rattles of a car blended with the chug of the motor as the sound came closer and closer.

"What if they find Gabe and we hear them trying to take him away?" Jerry croaked.

"I—I don't—"

Phil's words were cut short. Not ten feet away from the shed, the car motor died.

"You go around that way." The order came from the same voice they'd heard last night. "I'll look down by the water."

The clomp of footsteps resounded in their ears. Phil's chest ached. Then he realized he was holding his breath. What would happen if the couple discovered them?

"Roxie!" the man called out. "Here's some kids' bikes. You see them around anywhere?"

"Who're you trying to tell?" Roxie—as the man called her—was moving back in their direction. "I saw the old man's boat on the creek, but I wadn't about to announce it to the world."

"That means he's not out fishin'."

"Now how on earth did you figure that out?" she snarled and let out an oath. "You think you could check out that shed? I'll look in the other one."

Jerry's and Phil's eyes mirrored each other's fear. Could the man hear them breathing? Jerry's breath came in ragged spurts.

Sharp heels clicked on the concrete floor. *Cowboy boots.* Then quiet. The reek of cigarette smoke overpowered the smell of rust and oil.

In the moment of stillness they heard a second car. The steady drone became louder. Had the intruder heard it too? Suddenly the sound stopped. A car door slammed. A different voice asked, "Something I could help you with, sir?"

"Uh, well, ah . . . I'm just lookin' for a friend."

"Sorry. As you can see, I'm the only one here. All the shrimp boats are out—that is, all that'll run."

"Hugh," the woman called in a normal voice. "What's holdin' you up?"

The slam of a car door. A starter grinding, again and again.

"Well, uh, thanks anyway," Hugh said. Heels clicked. Outside, the car motor spit and sputtered to life. Then, rattling and chugging, it pulled away.

The fellow who had unknowingly rescued them mumbled, "Weird. Weird." With a sigh of relief, they heard his footsteps retreating.

"We got to get out of here," Jerry whispered. "I'm going to peek up."

Lifting just enough to catch a glimpse of the outside through the broad doorway, he dropped back in shock.

At the edge of the creek the maintenance man was talking to Gabe.

Jerry motioned for Phil to follow, and they edged to the doorway. Careful to stay out of sight, they listened.

"Now, Gabe," the man was saying, "don't tell me you slept here again last night. How many times we got to tell you about that? Now you go on up that creek to your house and sleep. Otherwise, we're gonna have to get the law after you."

"Oonuh seed dem buckruh heah?" Gabe was pleading. "Dey attuh me."

"Now come on, old man. Nobody's after you. What would anybody want with you?" He gave a weak laugh. "It's all in your head. You go on out and catch some fish. These islanders are waiting to buy them from you. And I've got work to do."

Phil swallowed around the hard knot in his throat. What Jerry said was true. Nobody believed Gabe. Instead, they threatened him with the law. No wonder Gabe believed the police would put him in jail.

The maintenance man swung himself onto a cruiser with *Seaworthy* printed on the side and disappeared below deck.

Quick as a flash the boys ran to the helpless-looking old man.

"We believe you, Gabe," Jerry said. "And we're going to help you. We know where the couple is staying, and we came to tell you we're making plans to get some of their clothes for you."

Gabe looked at them as if he wasn't clear on what he was hearing. He batted his eyes, and Phil couldn't help thinking how much the yellowish color of his eyeballs resembled a turtle's. A fine piece of twine cut into the thin skin of his forehead.

"What do you have that string on your head for, Gabe?" he asked.

"Dat gone cut muh headache."

Before Phil could respond, Jerry said, "I hope so, Gabe. I sure do hope so." He shot Phil a what-did-I-tell-you look.

"Can we go somewhere and talk?" Phil asked, sounding like one of those undercover men in the movies.

Gabe started down toward the bench where they'd first seen him mending the shrimp net. "Dey don' cyah iffen Uh heah een de daytime. Nyuse'tuh wu'k heah fuh wages w'en dey had de oshtuh factry." With his back as straight as a board, he eased himself down on the bench. Eben slunk around the corner of the shed, dripping little strings of saliva onto the sidewalk, and settled himself at Gabe's feet.

"Where were you when that couple was here?" Jerry asked.

"Oonuh see dat tall maa'sh grass?" He pointed up to the bank of the creek. "W'en Uh heah dat car en' seed it wuz green, Uh grab Eben en' scramble een de grass 'en squat down. Iffen Uh step on de root ub de cawdgrass Uh don' sink. Nawsuh." He nodded his head.

Was now the time to find out just what the couple wanted with Gabe? Phil wondered. Was Jerry thinking the same thing? Phil looked at his friend and nodded a go-ahead.

"Gabe," Jerry began, "like I told you, we know where the couple is staying on the island. They're at the campground where Phil's family is."

For the first time Gabe perked to attention. He mumbled something and started nodding his head in a

64

tell-me-more manner.

"See," Phil said, "we've got sisters, and we plan for them to help us get the clothes so your friend can conjure the man and woman."

For the first time they saw a hint of a smile creep over Gabe's face.

"But, Gabe," Jerry begged, "if we're going to help you, we need to know why the couple is after you."

Suddenly Gabe jerked his head to the right and then to the left. He lifted his frail body off the bench and scanned the creek. "Uh—Uh nyuse'tuh tawk 'bout it all de time," he said. "But now Uh skeert tuh." His hands started to tremble, and then his arms and shoulders began to shake. The shaking moved in waves over him until his entire body took on a violent tremor. His teeth clicked together in a frightening way.

Jerry leaned over and put his arm around the old man. "It's okay," he soothed. "Don't you worry. From now on all four of us are going to watch out for you."

"Jerry's right," Phil added. "We're going to stick by you. They could never do anything to all five of us."

Gradually his shaking subsided, and he began to look normal again.

"Now, Gabe," Jerry said. "You stay where there are other people around. You can go up to that dock behind the restaurant. There's always somebody there. Or, if you're out in your boat, stay across from those boat slips. Some of the owners use their boats like houses, and you could yell out to them for help."

"Will you do that, Gabe?" Phil asked. "While we get the clothes?"

He nodded his head. "Uh do dat. Uh sho do dat 'tell oonuh cum back wid de t'ing'."

"Besides," Jerry went on, "we're going to find somewhere for you to stay tonight."

Satisfied with Gabe's promise, they headed for their bikes.

"He about scared the living daylights out of me," Jerry said as soon as they got on their bikes.

"Me too. I didn't know what in the world was happening."

"I can't understand it." Jerry shook his head. "Whatever it is they want him for has him scared to death."

"It's a mystery all right," Phil said. "But tell me one thing. How are we going to find somewhere for him to sleep tonight?"

Jerry opened his mouth to answer his friend's question when a sight in the corner of his eye broke his train of thought. "Phil," he hissed through his teeth, "don't look back, but that green car— It's following us!"

Chapter 11

By the time the boys got back to the campground, their thoughts tumbled fast and furious. Having the couple spot them on their way home from the marina had really shaken them up. The green car had rattled alongside them at a snail's pace for what seemed forever.

Phil had glanced ever so quickly in their direction to see the man pointing at them and the big half-blonde woman staring out the window. His heart beat wildly. Had they remembered the bikes as being the same ones parked at the dock and now they knew who the riders were? Phil clenched his handle bars so tightly his hands felt as if they had gone to sleep. He knew Jerry was experiencing the same feeling.

But as quickly as the car had come upon them, it speeded up and creaked on toward the campsite.

"Whew!" Jerry let out a puff of breath that would move a sailboat. "That clinches it," he said. "We have to convince the girls to go after the possessions. The couple knows what we look like."

After a quick tour by their campsite for a refreshing soda, they set out to find Marcy and Sarah.

On the beach, they found them engrossed in their

sand castle.

"Now, remember, Jerry—cool and calm. We have to use psychology if we want to win them over."

"You're talking to the right fellow." He let a slow grin slip over his face.

Close enough for the sisters to hear, Phil whistled through his teeth. "Hey neat!" he exclaimed.

Marcy and Sarah exchanged glances and kept on patting the moist sand.

"You want us to get some water for your moat?" Phil asked.

Marcy dropped back on the sand and pulled her legs up Indian fashion. "Awh, come off it, will you?"

"Yeah," Sarah flashed her dark eyes up at them. "What do you want now?"

Phil plopped down on the other side of the castle with its turrets, and Jerry copied him. "The truth of the matter is," Phil said, "we thought we'd let you in on a really exciting mystery."

"That is," Jerry added, "if you can keep a secret."

Both girls stopped working and looked with suspicion at their brothers.

Phil waited for a lone walker to pass by. "It's like this. We're trying to help an old black man."

"Sarah," her brother said, "you know old Gabe Izzie buys fish from. Well, he's in trouble. Some people are after him."

"Who on earth would bother Gabe?" she asked.

"All we know is these people think Gabe knows where something is that they want," Jerry explained. "For some reason we don't know, Gabe says he can't tell. But if they try again to make him and he won't, there's no telling what they'll do to him."

"But," Phil went on, "we do know the people who are after him."

"And who is that?" Sarah asked, still a bit leery about what they were hearing.

Phil looked back and forth from Sarah to Marcy. "You know that weird couple you saw on the beach the other day?"

Sand castle and keeping secrets forgotten, Marcy almost yelled, "You mean the woman wrestler and the wiry man?"

"You've got to be kidding." Sarah let the sand she had scooped up slip from her hand.

"SSHHH—" the boys cautioned and looked around to see if anyone had heard. Thankful that the roar of the waves muffled sound, Phil said, "It's kind of complicated, and you won't understand it all, but—"

"Phil—" Marcy spoke through her teeth. "If you can understand it, we can understand it."

Phil put up his hand, face out. "Okay. Okay. No offense meant. It's just that Gabe has a friend who puts spells on people, and he can conjure these people and make them leave him alone *if*—"

"Have Mom and Dad heard you talk crazy?" Marcy interrupted.

"Wait a minute," Jerry tried to keep his voice quiet. "It's not like it sounds, Marcy. You can ask Sarah. She can tell you the older blacks on the sea islands are superstitious, and they believe in these things."

"I'll tell you what it sounds like," Marcy said. "It sounds like a job for the police."

"I thought that at first too," Phil said. "That's what I meant by saying it was complicated."

"The thing is," Jerry said, "nobody believes the poor

69

old man. He's been trying to sleep up where the shrimp boats dock, but they keep running him off."

"He's too scared to go to his home up Big Bay Creek," Phil added. "This couple has already been up there after him, but he managed to get away from them that time."

"So what do you want us to do?" Sarah asked.

The boys looked at each other and tried to decide who should answer Sarah's question. Phil nodded toward Jerry.

He took a deep breath before he said, "It's like this. Before the conjurer can do his work, he's got to have a piece of clothing belonging to the man and the woman."

Sarah started shaking her head halfway through Jerry's spiel."OH, NO. If you think—"

"But we can't do it," Phil said. "They know we've been with Gabe. They recognized our bicycles when they came up to the dock this morning looking for Gabe."

"And they slowed up by us as we rode home and glared at us." Jerry talked faster than usual. "If they saw you walking near their campsite, they wouldn't think anything about it."

"Taking people's clothes is stealing," Marcy said.

"If the couple's still around when the conjurer's through with them, we can give them back," Jerry told her.

"Who would want clothes with pins stuck all in them?" Sarah asked.

"I'll tell you what," Phil suggested. "Let's walk up toward their campsite. We scouted it out last night. The myrtle's thick, and they won't be able to see us."

"We want to finish our sand castle," Marcy said.

"We'll help you when we come back. Scout's honor." Jerry put his hand up.

"*Please!*" Phil begged.

Marcy looked at her brother. Never in her whole life

could she remember Phil ever saying *please* to her. He was really caught up in this thing. She turned to Sarah. "What do you think?" she asked.

"Oh, all right," she said, getting up and dusting off her hands. "But I'm scared."

For a moment the four of them stood staring down at the sand castle. It was as if Sarah spoke for all of them with her admission of fright.

Had knights in the days of real castles felt fear when they went to battle? Phil wondered. But then they had armor and swords. What could four bare-handed kids do against a giant of a woman and her sidekick?

"Okay." Jerry broke the reverie. "Let's head on up the beach."

Chapter 12

"If the timing isn't right, we won't try to get the possessions now," Phil promised as they hurried over the shell-covered beach. "We won't put you in danger."

"That's right," Jerry said. "We'll see what the situation is. They may not even be there."

"See," Phil explained, "we decided earlier they must keep their change of clothes in the car. They didn't even have their tent up when we were by here last night."

"I hope nobody bothers our sand castle while we're gone." Sarah looked over her shoulder to see a mother and her children admiring their handiwork.

"They're camped all the way up at the end," Phil said. "Going up to it from the beach side will give us the myrtle bushes for a screen."

Nearby a lady in a wide-brimmed hat stooped to pick up shells, and two teenage girls in matching shirts jogged by. Black shorebirds scattered out of their way in quick, stiff steps.

For a while they walked on in silence, dodging areas where sea water had snaked paths into the beach sand to make puddles.

Sarah wondered if others felt the way she did. Life

was going on around them just as it had before Phil and Jerry had shared their secret, and yet nothing seemed the same. She found herself wishing their brothers hadn't told them about Gabe being in danger. She was beginning to feel the way she did when she went in the hospital to have her tonsils out. It had been strange because she didn't have any say-so when the nurses gave her shots and the doctor put her to sleep. Here she was on the beach in the warm summer air, but she had that same anxious feeling she had had on the stretcher being wheeled into the hospital operating room.

"Sarah," Marcy questioned. "You okay?"

"Huh?" Sarah flinched. "Yeah. I guess so."

Quick to see the girls needed a pep talk, Jerry worked at making his voice sound cheery. "Botany Bay Island is on down this way. That's where we'll go one day for the big conchs. I've heard of people going there on foot when the tide's down. They swim across the inlets. But I sure wouldn't want to take that chance. Jeremy's Inlet is bad enough to cross. I'm not about to take on Frampton's."

Phil urged the chitchat along. They really needed to keep the girls' minds off getting the possessions. Otherwise, they might back out. "Didn't you say there's a man who takes people across to Botany Bay Island in his boat?" he asked. "Dad would go with us one day." He almost added "when we get Gabe taken care of," but he thought better of it just in time.

"There." Jerry pointed to their left. "That's where we should go in."

They turned up under the rustling palms and wind-bent oaks—sparse in this area—and headed toward the tangled jungle of myrtle, cactus, and jack vine.

The raucous cry of a bird made them jump. Sarah

73

grabbed Marcy's arm.

"Over here," Phil whispered. He bent over to ease under the low bushes. Jerry followed, with the girls close behind. In a small clearing they crouched to peer through at the campsite.

"The car's there," Jerry whispered. "But where are they?"

Phil kept his voice low. "If they're in the tent, they could hear the girls opening the car door."

"I'm not opening any car door." Sarah sounded as if she would start crying.

"*If* they're in the tent." Jerry was careful to keep his speech low and guarded. "I don't think they are. At least I don't think *she* is, or we'd hear her fussing. She'd argue with a tent pole."

"Where else would they be if the car's there?" Phil questioned.

"The beach—maybe."

"Jerry," Phil shot back. "We just came from the beach. Did you see them?"

"No, but we couldn't see beyond the pavilion. Or they could have walked to the store." His voice croaked in his effort to keep it low. He spoke out of the corner of his mouth to the girls behind them. "Now, remember," he said, "it's got to be one thing of hers and one of his."

The whine of mosquitoes around them increased, but nobody moved. All in a moment a twig cracked like a gunshot.

Suddenly Marcy sucked her lungs full of air, and fast as a bullet she whizzed by the crouching boys.

Their mouths hanging open, the three watched her dart behind the tent. With both hands she reached up and yanked clothing from a makeshift clothes line. She was making a desperate effort to retreat when the line collapsed, dragging the remaining clothing to the ground.

Like an enemy waiting for attack, the tent took on a life of its own. The opening flung back, exposing a big angry face with hair sticking out from her head like Medusa's.

"WHAT IN THE—?" the gaping mouth screamed.

The four were already fleeing for their lives when they heard the next bellow. "Hugh! Get out here! It's them dang kids again."

Yucca and cactus pricked their legs. Marcy's hair caught in a hanging vine. Jerry stumbled, leaving a shoe behind. Ahead, the others could see Phil's red hair zig zag as he dodged trees in his path.

Once on the open beach they ran like Jack being chased by the giant. Jerry yipped from the pain of running on shells without a left shoe. The clothing Marcy clutched fluttered behind her.

Phil, his breath like fire in his lungs, finally got the courage to look back. Two angry figures stood at the edge of the wooded area, their legs set like pirates ready to wield their daggers.

Chapter 13

Glad for the log marking their site, they scrambled up the sloping path for all they were worth. Inside the screened area, they plopped down huffing and puffing like steam engines. Beads of perspiration stood out on their faces. Little trickles ran down their foreheads into their eyes.

"G—Gosh, Marcy—" Jerry fought for breath. "You moved like lightning. What made you decide to go for it in such a hurry?"

"Mosquitoes," she huffed. "I didn't think it could be any worse."

They laughed nervously until she added, "But I was wrong."

"Boy!" Phil drew in a shivery breath of air. "Are we lucky! We're alive, and Mom and Dad aren't here to question us."

"Mom . . ." Marcy held her hand over her aching chest. "said they'd be . . . at the library . . . if we needed them."

Sarah took a giant breath and blew it out. "Did you see all those people on the beach gawking at us?"

Marcy nodded. "That means there are witnesses that we—I—stole. I should never have let you talk me into this." She glared at her brother.

Jerry bent over in the agony of nursing his foot. "I gotta have my shoe, or I'm skunked. Besides, it's murder around here without shoes."

"What size do you wear?" Phil's breath was coming easier now. "You can wear some of mine."

"Nine E."

"Uh—oh. Too wide. I'm nine and a half B."

"You'll never convince *me* to go back for it." Marcy set her mouth tight.

"OH, NO!" All eyes turned to Sarah. She held her hand over her mouth and stared at the clothes Marcy still clutched.

"Of all the stupid—" Phil's face showed disgust.

Marcy looked down. The biggest bra she had ever seen in her entire life dangled from her hand. The other piece in her fist was a pair of red and white striped boxer shorts. In her haste she had grabbed the couple's underwear.

Jerry hollered, "For crying out loud!"

Sarah giggled.

"Well," Marcy fought back, her anger nearing tears, "it's not like I had all the time in the world to pick and choose, you know." With the three of them grinning around her, Marcy felt her anger wane enough to say, "At least they're clean."

"You did good, Marcy," Sarah consoled. "I didn't even see the clothesline until you attacked it."

"Me either," Jerry said as if in apology for his earlier behavior. "And that's just what you did. You attacked it. Did you see that thing swing down?"

They washed their sweaty hands and faces and got drinks. They were sitting around the picnic table when

Jerry gulped down a big swallow and pointed across the campsite to the far road of the loop. "Look!" he cried. The old green trap of a car sputtered along the dirt road toward the exit of the park. "And they're pulling the boat!"

"Maybe they're leaving." Sarah's voice was hopeful. "And we can be through with this crazy idea."

"Or maybe they're going after Gabe," Jerry said. "We gotta hurry up and get back to him."

"Yeah, and give him the—the *stuff*," Phil added.

Marcy thought she saw a hint of a smile on her brother's face. She felt her dander rising again. "Now, Phil Dunlap, don't you think for one darn moment you're going to use us to do your dirty work and then shut us out."

"Who said anything about shutting you out?" he shot back.

"I don't want to go with them," Sarah said. "I want to finish our sand castle. Anyway, it's smelly down at the dock."

"Suppose Jerry and I go deliver the goods. If we don't come back, you two can tell people to look for us on Big Bay Creek."

"Or, we may just keep where you are a secret." Marcy clamped her teeth together.

"Tell you what," Jerry said. "Meet us on the beach at sunset, and you'll learn as much as we know about the whole thing."

Satisfied with Jerry's promise, the girls headed back to their sand castle.

"I'm glad you said make it above the high-tide mark, Sarah, or it would have been washed away. Look. It's just like we left it."

"Almost," Sarah agreed. "It's dried out some, but we

78

can fix that." She dropped down and started digging a hole. As she scooped out the coarse sand, it became damper and damper until a little pocket of water welled into the hole.

Soon they were lost in adding moisture to the drying areas and choosing special shells for walkways and decorations. Though neither wanted to talk about it, Marcy caught Sarah sneaking glances up the beach where earlier they had made their life-or-death chase. It was good to know the couple had left the campground—at least for now.

Still, something kept repeating itself in Marcy's mind like the waves returning to shore. Phil had said "If we don't come back, look for us on Big Bay Creek," and she had made a joke of it. What they were all involved in now was no joke.

A sudden breeze whipped up from the ocean. The smell of the sea was heavy with brine. The horizon lay as gray as a camp blanket. Gulls shrieked and swooped toward the choppy water, now a gray reflection of the sky.

For the first time Marcy noticed how deserted the beach was. She looked at Sarah. Her friend's face was in half shadow as she bent over the turret, patting moisture into it with both hands. Marcy took a deep breath. Was the couple taking their boat to Big Bay Creek where Phil and Jerry were headed? If the boys really turned up missing, how long should they keep their secret? If she and Sarah were forced to tell, should they include about stealing the clothes?

It was nearing noon, the warmest time on the beach. But, for some reason, she felt cold. She looked up to search for the sun under the haziness. Her T-shirt offered little warmth. Somehow, though, she knew even the warm-up suit she'd brought along wouldn't thaw out the hard, cold lump inside her.

Chapter 14

Feeling braver now that they'd seen the couple leave the campground, Phil and Jerry detoured by way of their campsite to retrieve Jerry's lost shoe. As they expected, nothing gave any evidence the ranting couple had ever been there.

With the underclothes twisted tightly in a plastic grocery bag, they headed to the dock area and to Gabe. All the while they kept a watch for the old green car that might pull alongside them at any moment.

Each felt relief flooding through them when they saw Gabe in his boat. They stood straddling their bikes and took in the scene. If they hadn't experienced the turmoil of the past days, the picture could have been captured for a vacation poster to lure visitors to the island. Anchored just off the marsh grass on the opposite side of Big Bay Creek, the boat swayed gently with the movement of the water. A gray light fell over the marsh grass with its shades of green and wrapped around Gabe and Eben, his head hanging lazily over the side of the boat.

"Gosh," Phil exclaimed, "they look like they're carved out of wood."

They watched as Gabe threw out his shrimp net. It

swept over the water like a broad-winged bird, then settled and sank.

"Let's see if we can call him over and let him know we have the clothes."

They parked their bikes and darted on the other side of the tall fence. Taking the liberty of walking out on the pier of the condominiums, they passed the nearby marina with its gift shop and restaurant. Within calling distance, Jerry hailed Gabe and held up the plastic bag with the clothes.

Gabe began to pull on his net, drawing it in. It shaped up like a balloon as he gathered it into his boat.

"He's got shrimp," Jerry said.

Then in a mechanical way, Gabe pulled up his anchor. With it in his boat, he lifted his paddle and sliced into the water on one side and then the other with barely a ripple.

The boys hurried back to the spot where Gabe always docked his boat and met him eagerly. In the bottom of the boat, shrimp moved in the net.

As usual, Gabe did not change his expression as he tied his boat to a piling and came toward them. Jerry opened the bag for him to peek at the *personal possessions*.

The fine skin of his forehead furrowed. "Uh see kin Uh fine de man." He reached for the bag and stuck it inside his shirt. "Uh sho 'bliged," he said. "Sho am."

"Gabe," Jerry hesitated. "Are you going to take the clothes now? Does the man live up Big Bay Creek?"

"Yaas'suh. Sho am. En' dat weh 'e lib."

"Could Phil and I go with you?" he blurted out.

Phil couldn't believe what he was hearing. He would really like to go up the creek in a boat, but with things the way they were—

Gabe pondered. "Tell'e wuh." He scratched his head.

"Uh gone pit dese swimp een de buckit. Oonuh tek 'um tuh e granmudduh en' ax huh kin'e go."

"All right!" Jerry cried. "Izzie'll let us go. I know she will—long as we have on life preservers."

"Ent got but one," Gabe said as he stepped back into his boat and began to scoop up the shrimp.

"There are plenty under Izzie's house." Jerry fairly hopped with excitement.

Gabe handed him the shrimp. "Tell huh go 'head en' pit 'um een de freezuh. Uh gone bring huh sum mo'."

"Okay." With Phil following, Jerry dashed to his bike, hung the bucket on his handlebar, and they were off.

"Jerry," Phil said as they pedaled up Palmetto Boulevard, "we should have told Gabe about the couple taking their boat out. They may be on Bay Creek too you know."

"Uh–oh. You're right. I plumb forgot, but we'll be right back."

Jerry seemed so happy Phil wondered if he'd forgotten what a threat the couple was to them at this very moment. The green car could run them down on the road. *Hit and run.* You read about it all the time in the papers.

True to Jerry's word, Izzie—between playing her cards—agreed they could go.

"We'll get life preservers from under the house," Jerry said, "as soon as I bag these shrimp Gabe sent you for the freezer. He's going to bring you some more."

"Wonderful!" Izzie responded.

"Are you sure the boys will be all right in Gabe's little Trust My God boat?" one of the ladies asked between a *six no trump* bid and a *pass.*

"Jerry knows the waters around Edisto Island better than I do," Izzie said. "They'll be okay."

Phil heard laughter on the way out, and somebody said, "Your lead, Maisie."

With the life preservers on Phil's bike rack and Gabe's empty bucket dangling from Jerry's handlebars, they started back.

Still feeling uneasy about the situation, Phil said, "I don't guess my parents will mind if I go. They're not here for me to ask."

"They won't mind since Izzie gave permission," Jerry assured him. "Anyway, we won't be gone long."

Gabe and Eben waited for them in the boat. With bikes parked behind the shed, they headed out. The smell

of shrimp was strong as they strapped on life jackets and stepped into the small boat. Jerry took the seat in the bow, facing the others. Phil sat on the middle board seat, and Gabe in his rowing spot at the rear with Eben nestled at his feet.

With easy strokes Gabe moved them up the swiftly running creek. Soon the marina with its sheds and the scattering of houses along the creek gave way to lonely stretches of marshland on either side. Wind-ravaged trees stuck up from tidal flats. Gray-black moss hung over decayed limbs.

"The tide's going out," Jerry called out. He had turned

to face the flow of the creek and perched like a dragon head on a Viking warship.

Along the mud-caked shore, a white egret stood on one leg, then spread his wings and flew over the marsh grass.

"That was neat!" exclaimed Phil.

"Look at those pelicans." Jerry pointed to the black silhouettes against the gray sky. "Watch how they change formations."

"Yeah," Phil called. "One changes position, and they all do."

Suddenly Phil felt the boat turning. Gabe was rowing them into a narrow wedge of the creek with a firm-looking mound of hard earth. Sitting in the center of the small hill was an unpainted shack. Board shutters covered the windows. The door was closed up tight.

Before they knew it, Gabe had beached the boat and was stepping out.

"Uh be right back." He headed over the sloping ground to the marshes where a hump-shouldered man poked a long stick into the mucky-looking flat.

When the man caught sight of Gabe, he pulled up the stick. A small crab clung to it. He tapped his stick on the side of his bucket to loosen its hold and stepped up to meet Gabe.

With a fast exchange of Gullah, the men walked toward the shack. The man's stooped posture was a sharp contrast to Gabe's tall stature.

"Is that the conjure man?" Phil asked. "I didn't know his back was so hunched over."

"That's him all right. You couldn't tell it so much when he was sitting in the boat."

They watched as the man they'd seen at the Indian

Mound led Gabe into his house. He opened the door, and suddenly the two of them seemed to be swallowed up by a black hole before the door closed again.

"Look at the fiddler crabs." Jerry pointed to the small crabs scurrying sideways over the mudflat beside the boat. "They burrow into the mud to get away from the birds that feed on them. If you can get close enough to see, they have funny-looking popeyes that sit out on their heads like glasses." He leaned over the edge of the boat and peered at them.

Was Jerry not thinking about what might be going on inside the house? Phil wondered. The fiddler crabs were interesting all right, but at the moment he was more concerned about the voodoo thing. Would there be a big corncob doll, he wondered, with wild hair wrapped in a bra and a skinny one with red-striped boxer shorts? Was Jerry not curious, or did he just want to block out the weird feeling of that place?

Finally, the door opened and Gabe came back to join them.

"Will he do it, Gabe?" Jerry asked.

"'E uh do it awright. But it gone tek uh w'ile."

"Gabe," Phil drew on his courage and asked, "Does he really make dolls and stick pins in them?"

"'E mek de doll awright," he said nodding.

"Where does he keep them?" Jerry asked.

"Een de draw'r. 'E pit 'um een de daa'k draw'r."

Phil shuddered. He couldn't believe he'd actually been a part of something like this. Nobody in New York would even believe him if he told them. Maybe that was for the best.

Back on the main part of Big Bay Creek, Gabe continued to row up creek. Phil looked at the back of Jerry's head. Wasn't he concerned they were still headed away from the dock? Had he forgotten the couple may be on this creek at this very instant? They could come blasting up this way any minute with their motor boat. They could crash into Gabe's little boat, leaving them unconscious to wash out to sea. They should tell Gabe about them so they could turn around and get back to safer quarters.

"Where are we going now?" Jerry's question passed Phil on the way to Gabe.

"Up by muh house. Uh needs tuh see 'bout muh chickin."

Jerry turned all the way around. "Hold up, Gabe. We've got something to tell you."

A feeling of relief swept over Phil. Jerry hadn't forgotten about the couple being on the loose. Maybe now they would turn around and head back toward the dock. With all his heart he hoped so. The sight before them was a vast marshland without a living soul to hear a cry for help.

Chapter 15

"What we need to tell you, Gabe—" Jerry planted his feet on the bottom of the boat to steady himself. "That man and woman—we saw them leaving the campground earlier today. They were pulling a motor boat and could come after you—or us—on the water."

"Dat how dey cum 'fo'. But dey ent likely tuh bodduh me w'ile oonuh wid me."

Gabe's explanation seemed to satisfy Jerry. After all, hadn't the two of them told Gabe the same thing by the shed? It *would be* difficult for the couple to handle all of them on land. But on water? Try as he might, Phil couldn't put his mind at rest.

Suddenly a plan for land began to formulate in his mind. There'd never been a doubt he could outrun them. Wasn't he on the track team at school? Besides, they'd all proved that when they got caught taking the *possessions*. But running would leave Gabe behind. The best bet seemed to rush them head on. Ordinarily he might tackle his foe, but tackling that woman would be out of the question. That would be like trying to bring down a player for the Chicago Bears. Jumping on her back and hanging on like a leech would probably be the best strategy. Her hands would be so busy trying to pry him off she wouldn't have time to grab Gabe. In the meantime, Jerry could handle the little guy. He could even tickle him into submission. Tickling was the only way he was ever able to get the upper hand on an older neighbor kid who sometimes liked to bully him. That made his muscles limp as a dish rag. For a moment he almost felt light-hearted.

Just as quickly he sobered. That plan would work on land. But on water? And in Gabe's little Trust My God? They wouldn't stand a chance.

The grinding of a starting motor jerked Phil out of his reverie. Jerry heard it too. He whipped around. The boat was hidden from view around the bend in the creek, but whoever was there raced the motor repeatedly, then gave it full throttle.

With a feeling of panic, Phil watched for Gabe's reaction. In a succession of strokes on the left side, Gabe made an effort to turn them toward shore.

At that moment a speedboat barreled around the bend. With a quick wave of his hand, the pilot zoomed past, leaving a sloshing trail of churning water.

"Hole on!" Gabe called. Their boat rocked, then pitched and rolled in the boat's wake. Phil followed Jerry's lead and dropped to the bottom of the boat. He felt the strong smell of shrimp seep into his clothing as he hung on for dear life.

Gabe had shoved his paddle under the middle seat, and now he clutched the sides of his boat. One leg fastened over Eben to keep him from being thrown overboard.

"That's against the law!" Jerry shouted as soon as the waves began to subside. He raised his fist against the inconsiderate man who was now only a speck in the distance.

The wave action created by the speeding boat had washed them toward the side of the creek. Unruffled now that the intruder had not been the dreaded couple, Gabe retrieved his paddle and pushed them off. Once again he took up the rhythm of leaning from side to side, dipping the blade tip of his paddle and pulling it back with a gentle stroke. They still headed upstream.

Phil's mind was not so settled. The boat could just as easily have been the beige one they'd seen behind the green car. It could have rammed them broadside and been called an accident. They needed to get off the water. He had to make Jerry and Gabe listen to reason.

Sooner than Phil figured, Gabe paddled to the right, entering another tributary of Big Bay Creek. The tidal smell was strong. Like the voyage up to the conjurer's house, they went until the water ran out.

From where Gabe beached the boat, they saw a leaning shack. It stood on a rise above the high-water mark. Sturdy driftwood limbs propped up the right side. Like the other house, wooden shutters covered the windows. On the tiny porch, tin cans held orange and black flowers like the wild ones blooming in Izzie's yard. Several chickens and a rooster stepped and scratched about. Seeing Gabe, they cackled and clucked. Jerry turned to Phil, excitement showing in his face.

The three stepped out of the boat to cross a narrow ditch onto dry, hard earth. The sun had cracked the ground like lines in a crockery bowl. Yet a short distance away muddy marsh flats reeked of sea water dregs.

Gabe turned to Jerry. "Oonuh knows how tuh prime dat pump en' raise up de watuh?"

91

"I think so. I did it at camp."

"Do dat den." Gabe handed him the bucket from the boat. "Watuh Eben en' de chickin." He climbed the uneven steps and went into the house. Phil was surprised the door had not been locked.

Jerry found a rusty cup tucked beneath the pump handle. It held a bit of water for priming. Cautiously he poured a few drops and pumped up and down on the handle. Nothing but creaks and groans.

"That's not enough water," Phil said. "Pour some more. If you run out, we can get some from the creek. I'll bet it tastes like creek water anyway. Here, let me," he said, reaching for the cup.

Phil poured and Jerry pumped, and soon water flowed into the bucket. By the time they got water to Eben and the chickens, Gabe was out again throwing handfuls of corn on the ground. "Needs tuh pen de chickin up," he said. "Gatuh got one las' week."

"Alligator?" Phil looked around. At least the house had a cleared area around it so they could see one if it started coming for them.

"Cum een de house. We needs sump'n' tuh eat."

Phil and Jerry looked at each other and then their watches. They had completely forgotten lunch, and here it was midafternoon.

As soon as their eyes became accustomed to the dim light, they took in the meager surroundings of the two-room house. The open fireplace gave off a kind of burned wood smell. Above it, the brick and mantelpiece were streaked with smoke. A cot was pushed against the wall in the small room. On the floor beside it lay a pair of old brown slippers with the backs worn down. A shelf above the bed held a bottle of rubbing alcohol and some medicine bottles.

In the kitchen Gabe had pushed open the wooden shutter. Light flooded through the screenless window. A pipe ran up from a small black stove through the roof of the house. Gabe was busying himself building a fire. He lifted the eye of the stove and dropped in dry moss and bits of driftwood from a cardboard box on the floor. He leaned down, opened a damper under the bottom, and lit the fire. Soon it crackled and popped.

"Look een de hen house out back en' git de aig." He nodded his head toward Jerry, and Phil followed him out the door. In seconds they were back with four of the biggest brown eggs they had ever seen.

Gabe fried salt pork in a black frying pan, and the smell of it replaced all other unpleasant ones up the marshy creek.

Phil gave an "Mmmm" and Jerry smacked his lips as they watched Gabe. The bacon ready, he poured the drippings into a tin cup and filled the pan with bread slices, turning and toasting them to a warm, soft brownness. When the fire beneath the pan seemed too hot, Gabe lifted it off the stove eye until the heat regulated itself and then set it down again. Next he broke three eggs into a bowl and whipped them up. Pouring some of the fat drippings back into the pan, he scrambled up the eggs for their sandwiches.

Jerry had brought in the other chair from the bedroom, and they gathered around the rickety table.

"Don't you have any chairs besides these straight ones, Gabe?" Phil asked.

"Nawsuh." He reached for three glasses and a big bottle of Coke from his white enamel cabinet. "Odduh kine mek 'e lazy."

"So that's why you stand up so straight?" Jerry asked. "Mom's always telling me if I don't quit slouching when I sit, my spine's going to grow crooked, but I didn't believe her."

The three of them laughed together. Then Gabe bowed his head and closed his eyes. They did the same.

"T'ank'e Lawd fuh de hep Oonuh sunt me. Amen."

A good feeling passed over Phil. He looked up to see Jerry smiling. He was glad they were helping Gabe—whatever the risk.

Jerry chomped down on his bacon and egg sandwich. "You're a good cook, Gabe."

"T'ank'e. Uh duz tol'rable."

"Have you always lived here?" Phil asked.

"Long as Uh 'membuh. De house pass down tuh me." In the next breath he said, "Yaas'suh, dat spell gwine sho wu'k. Uh gone be free."

While they ate, Gabe heated a pan of water on top of his little stove. Now he slipped their dishes into it and sent the food he'd put aside for Eben out by the boys.

Jerry had just scraped Eben's food in his pan by the pump when they heard the boat coming up the creek at full speed.

He was about to holler to Gabe when he saw the beige boat twisting toward them. Instead, he and Phil lit out to the marsh.

"Of all the—" Phil sank to his ankles in the sucking mud. One look at Jerry's face told him his friend was in the same boat. Disgusting ooze suctioned them to the bottom of the mudflat, wherever that was.

What they heard next made the mud seem mild. The coarse voice of the woman traveled over the water to them. "See them blasted kids? They're up there with the

94

old man."

The sucking mud had caught them so off guard, they hadn't ducked down. Then, to their surprise, the boat lurched into a careening U-turn and zipped back in the other direction.

For a moment the boys stood dumbfounded. Gabe had told them at the dock he had hidden in the marsh grass where no one could follow him. He was right about that.

Scrunching their faces like a spoonful of castor oil was being held in front of their noses, they grabbed at clumps of stiff saw grass and pulled until with a loud slurp they reclaimed their feet.

"I guess it was all for the good they did see us." Jerry's shoes squished as he tried to wipe off gunk at the edge of the marsh.

"Yeah. There's no telling what would have happened to Gabe if they hadn't seen us. But I'll tell you something else, Jerry. If we don't soon find out what they want with Gabe, we may not be able to help him when the time comes."

"I just don't want to get him upset again. But we're getting closer. I know we are."

"I hope you're right." Phil looked down at the muddy water oozing from his grubby shoes and made a face.

Chapter 16

Outside the house they pulled off their muck-covered shoes and socks and went in to find Gabe. They stood still, letting their eyes become accustomed to the dimness. Everything was deadly quiet.

"Gabe?" Jerry's voice sounded hollow.

"Do you think he heard the boat coming and ran out the back to the marsh?" Phil asked.

Silence.

"Let's go see," Jerry said. "We need to get off this creek. They may change their plans and come back."

Pleased Jerry was seeing things his way, Phil agreed. "We'd be trapped where we are now. Gabe and the conjure man may be able to move over these marshes, but you and I can't. We just proved that."

They had started out when Jerry caught sight of Gabe's arm sticking from under his cot. He was making an effort to crawl out.

"Good heavens, Gabe!" Jerry exclaimed. "That's the worst possible place you could hide. We always looked under the beds first when we used to play hide and seek in the house."

How, Phil wondered, could Jerry compare *this* hide-

and-seek game with these strangers to a childhood game of fun.

"The couple—they saw us," Phil told Gabe. "They said something about those blasted kids being up here and whipped the boat around. We don't know if they're planning to come back, but we should get down to the dock around other people."

On his feet again, Gabe trembled as he straightened up and placed a shaking hand on his lower back.

Phil took a deep breath. He had to take a chance. "I'll sure be glad when you can tell us why the couple is after you, Gabe."

Gabe wrapped his long arms around his body, and his face took on a frightened look. "Lak Uh say 'fo', Uh nyuse'tuh tell muh story all de time. Now Uh skeert ub Melia."

Phil felt like an attorney drilling his client. "You're not making sense, Gabe." He threw his hands up in frustration.

"Well, just tell us one thing, Gabe." Jerry stepped over and put his arm around Gabe's shoulders. "Who's Melia?"

He looked around as if to make sure no one else was in the room, clasped his hands together to keep them steady, and whispered. "*Sh—She uh gos'*."

· · · · ·

The trip back down the creek was different from the one they'd taken up. They had forced Gabe to tell them Melia was a ghost. Hearing that cast a spell of gloom over an already scary situation. They hadn't wanted to hear more. At least not in this spot.

Phil had been doubtful about going up Big Bay Creek

in the first place. Now he was sure it had been a mistake. For the second time the couple had seen him and Jerry blocking their efforts to get at Gabe. They had put themselves in danger.

The smell of their shoes, the boat, and the marsh in general added to the queasiness of the feelings sloshing about inside him.

The flow of the creek was with them now, and Gabe's paddling seemed all the more effortless and light. Yet even that added to the eeriness of their movement. It was almost like watching a movie of explorers going into uncharted places. . . . *And, alligators.* . . . He'd heard they were around these islands. Gabe had given proof of that. Could one turn over their small boat?

Suddenly a gull swooped, cried a warning, and plunged for a fish. Phil jumped. He was glad Jerry did not see him act so edgy. But his friend was strangely quiet too. What was he thinking?

By the time they reached the dock, the sky had taken on a rusty look. Shrimp boats had already come in, and now this side of the restaurant seemed pretty much deserted.

Just as Gabe paddled the boat to the piling, Jerry broke a long silence. "Gabe, you shouldn't stay down here tonight. If you'll meet me and Phil at the pavilion at sunset, I know a good spot close to us."

Phil whipped around toward Jerry, his face a question mark.

"Don't worry," Jerry consoled his friend. "Those myrtles around that campground are so thick a whole army could hide in them."

On the way back, the boys kept their usual lookout for the green wreck of a car with the tall, heavy-set woman and the wimpy little man in the passenger seat beside her. Several times the sound of a heavy motor or the rattle of an oncoming vehicle stopped their breaths, but it always turned out to be the UPS delivery van or a garbage truck.

Two boys on bicycles would be easy to spot from a distance. If they were accosted here, the best thing to do would be to drop their bikes like lit firecrackers and run between the houses toward the beach. They couldn't follow them there.

"Hey, Phil—" Jerry broke his thoughts. "I'm stopping by Izzie's to get cleaned up. I'll be at the pavilion at sunset to meet Gabe."

Phil pedaled on at a quicker pace. A faint outline of the moon over the graying ocean waited for the sun to go down.

The now familiar campsite looked good to him. He found Marcy and Sarah watching *Jeopardy*.

"Where're Mom and Dad?" he asked.

"At the store," his sister answered without taking her eyes from the set. "Phew!" she added as he passed by. "You stink."

"Where's Jerry?" asked Sarah.

"At Izzie's." Phil grabbed a change of clothes and made a quick getaway to the bath house shower. He remembered their promise that the girls could join them on the beach at sunset, but right now he didn't want to have to answer any questions.

At supper Phil was still in a quiet mood. As usual his dad was caught up in history. "Everywhere I go," he said, "the islanders want to make sure I get information on Hephzibah Jenkins Townsend. It seems she had a narrow escape as an infant during the American Revolution but grew up to be a strong-willed woman who, among other things, started the Baptist church on the Island."

"Do you tell them you're concentrating on the Civil War this go-'round?" his wife asked.

"I try to, but you know me and history."

His wife smiled.

There was so much Phil wanted to share with his parents. But he dared not mention the ride up Big Bay Creek. That would involve telling about Gabe. He and Jerry just weren't ready for that yet. He hoped they wouldn't find out from Izzie before he told them. Maybe she wouldn't remember giving permission since she was so wrapped up in her bridge game.

He excused himself early to walk down to the pavilion to meet Jerry. On his way by Marcy he said, "You and Sarah can come down to our sleeping spot after awhile if you want to. We're going to tell some stories."

"What a lovely idea to invite the girls." His mother looked at his dad as if to say "Our son is turning into a really nice young man after all."

With a pang of guilt, Phil headed to the beach and took a right toward the pavilion.

Jerry was already there, and the two of them stood at the edge of the parking area watching cars turn down the main street.

"Is Palmetto Boulevard the only road in and out of the island?" Phil asked.

"It used to be. There's Jungle Road now. It joins up with Palmetto Boulevard on around from the dock area and leads back into the highway just beyond where we turned off to go to the Indian Mound." For a moment Jerry looked as if he was deep in thought. "A criminal could get away on that other road if that's what you're wondering."

"Here comes Gabe." Phil stepped out for a better view.

They watched the straight, thin figure move toward them. His legs and feet seemed to carry him along in a gliding way. Eben loped behind, his tail tucked between his legs.

"What's Gabe got under his arm?" Phil asked.

"Beats me." Jerry stepped aside to allow a lady with two children to get up the steps to the gift shop.

As Gabe drew nearer, they could see that the bundle he was carrying looked like a big gray pillow.

Seeing them staring, Gabe gave a hint of a smile. "Dis muh bed. It moss off de tree. Uh soke it een salt watuh en' dries it een de sun. It be saa'f."

"Neat!" Jerry leaned down and rubbed Eben's head, and they started up the beach. One late swimmer bobbed at the edge of the ocean. Scattered walkers and shell seekers gave them passing glances.

"Uh lef' 'e granmudduh sum mo' swimp on de way by High Tide," Gabe said.

"That's great! We'll help eat them." Jerry grinned.

As they went along, Phil felt himself scouring the beach area and the bordering myrtle bushes like a security guard watching over the president of the United States.

At the moment they spotted their path on the dune, Marcy and Sarah appeared and raced over to them.

By way of introduction to Gabe, Jerry said, "Marcy's the one who got the clothes. She's Phil's sister. Sarah's mine."

"Uh know it." Gabe looked at Phil's red hair and freckles and then at Marcy's. "'E spit'n image. Jes lak dese two." He pointed to the dark hair of Jerry and Sarah.

"Will your dog bite?" Sarah stooped down.

"Nutt'n' but bittle." Gabe showed his teeth in a grin.

Glad to see him more relaxed than when they left him earlier, Jerry pointed to a small clearing up in the myrtles. "We thought you and Eben could sleep here," he said.

Gabe stepped and tossed down his bedding. "Jes so Uh don' hab tuh sleep wid de moon een muh face. Dat mek 'e go crazy."

Marcy and Sarah looked at one another in amusement, and then watched Eben curl himself on the edge of the moss bed. "Mosquitoes are going to eat you up under there," Marcy said.

"Dey don' bodduh me nun. Sumtime een de summuh Uh bu'ns uh ole tiah or rag wid kyarrysene 'kase Uh don' lak 'um winin' 'roun'."

Marcy squinched her nose.

"Well," Jerry said, "if they decide to bother you, you can move farther out in the breeze—after it gets good and dark."

"Come on," Phil suggested, "let's sit on this log and talk."

When they were settled, Sarah asked, "Gabe, have you always lived on Edisto?"

"Bawn heah. Nebbuh eben cross Dawhoo Bridge." Gabe emitted a kind of cackle. "Uh fish on de Woopin' Islant Crick by de bridge 'fo' en' see it draw up fuh de boats."

Phil couldn't believe Gabe was talking so much. If only they could keep him going, they had a good chance of finding out what they wanted to know. Then, like the sting of a mosquito, the thought hit him: What if their parents came down and found Gabe with them? They'd have no choice but to explain the situation. Just as quickly as that thought had entered his head, another brighter one took over.

Chapter 17

"Just for the record," Marcy said, dumping the sleeping bags at their feet, "we are not your slaves."

"I told you we can't take a chance on having Mom or Dad come down to check on us. That's why I asked you to go up and tell them we're fine."

"Yeah," Jerry echoed. "Who said doing us a favor of bringing our sleeping bags, as long as you're there anyway, makes you a slave?"

The word *slave* seemed to prompt Gabe to speak. "Muh granmudduh wuh libbed tuh de Brick House Plantation brung tuh de islant uh slabe. Huh fambly cum frum African king."

Jerry gasped. "So that's why you stand so straight and tall—you got a king's blood. It's not because you never slouch in chairs. Wait till I tell my mom that."

Tell his mom. Like the repetition of the incoming tide, telling his parents kept repeating itself in Phil's mind. At least Jerry's parents weren't here for him to keep deceiving, and Izzie seemed far too preoccupied with her bridge to be interested. If they could find out what they needed to know tonight—

"Okay," Jerry was saying, "who's going to tell the first

story?"

"Yunnuh heah 'bout de slabe?" Gabe asked. Before anyone could answer, he was off—telling how families in Africa were torn apart in the taking of slaves to America.

"Slow up, Gabe," Marcy responded to the clipped, quacking speech. "I don't want to miss anything. What does *yunnuh* mean anyway?"

Jerry beat him in the reply. "It means *Do you want to*. He says 'Do you want to hear about the slaves?'" He laughed. "I hate to tell you, Marcy, but you—and Phil—talk funny too."

Everybody laughed. "Say *water*, Marcy," Sarah said.

They all had fun listening to the various sounds as each of them repeated *water*. Finally, they came to the conclusion that Southerners' 't's sound like 'd's.

"That's enough of that," Phil said. "Let Gabe tell his story."

"Yaas'suh." Gabe started up again, obviously pleased with the attention he was getting. "Muh granmudduh uh house serbant tuh de Brick House Plantation. She 'membuh w'en de big guns shoot."

"You mean the War Between the States?" Sarah asked. "That was almost a hundred and fifty years ago."

"Yaas'suh. Dat 'bout de time dem Yankees cum down heah." Gabe sounded like the thought had put a bad taste in his mouth.

Sarah and Marcy giggled until they felt Jerry's foot poking them to keep quiet. Finding out he was talking to two *Yankees* may put a damper on his stories. They didn't want that.

In the moonlight Phil saw Gabe lace his fingers together the way he had done at the dock. "De Maussuh ub de Brick House, 'e sont 'is fambly tuh de Up Country w'en

de waa' staa'tt. Den 'e go off hissef tuh fight. 'E weh de gray."

"That means he joined the Confederate Army. Right, Gabe?" Jerry wanted to make sure the others understood.

"Dat right. De Nawt', dey blue; de Sout', gray. Anyways, de fambly tek wuh de could wid 'um. Dey don' hab no way tuh carry de big stuff wuh been brung cross de ocean on de ship. De Maussuh 'e tell de feel han' tuh stay en' tek cyah de lan'. 'E sont de house serbant Up Country wid de fambly. De house serbant dey glad 'kase dey lub dere fambly, en' dey knows dey be look attuh. But muh granmudduh she don' wunnah go. She lub dat fambly too, en' dey lub huh; but huh chillun all feel han', en' she skeert she wone nebbuh see 'um no mo'. She beg de Maussuh leh huh stay."

"The Union soldiers didn't bother the blacks, did they, Gabe?" asked Phil. "After all, they were fighting to free them."

"Dey ent gone shoot 'um. Nawsuh. But pret soon de sodjuh cum t'ru, en' dey tek all de bittle fuh deysefs. De peoples lef' behime be hongry. De sodjuh tek de cow en' de chickin sqawkin en' flutterin frum de coop. Dey tu'n out de hog een de feel. Muh granmudduh en' huh peoples be hongry too."

Gabe stopped, and the whooshing of the waves filled the silence. First, the sound came in kind of gathering force, then a burst.

"Did her master let her stay?" asked Sarah.

Gabe's voice took on the softness of the night. "Sho did. But 'fo' 'e lef, 'e tek huh out by de crick onduh de big oak wid de moss hangin' down. En' 'e say low weh noboddy cyan' heah. 'E say 'Delia'—dat huh name—Delia. 'E say 'Delia, oonuh gone be de one hang 'roun' heah de longes'. Uh not eben gone tell muh fambly wuh I gone tell'e. Dem Yankees ebbuh try tuh mek any my fambly tawk, dey don' know nutt'n.' "

Again, Gabe stopped. The lull between waves made a mysterious quiet.

"Go on, Gabe," Phil urged.

The quiet stretched. Things around them took on a ghostlike appearance in the moonlight. Even the girls' sand castle with its markings of shells looked like some prehistoric sea animal crawling ashore.

"It's okay, Gabe," Jerry comforted. "We're friends, You can tell us anything."

"Yeah," Phil agreed. "We asked you to spend the night with us so we could protect you. Besides, the more we know, the better we can help take care of you."

"Uh knows oonuh muh fr'en'." He seemed weak and tired. "Lak Uh say, nyuse'tuh tell 'bout dis all de time. But Uh skeert sence de buckruh attuh me."

Phil and Jerry looked at one another. They couldn't let him stop now.

"Gabe," Phil asked, "do you remember when we were at your house and you told us Melia was a ghost?"

Gabe caught his breath and let it out in a slow shaky way. "Uh— 'membuh."

"Will you tell us about her?" he asked.

Chapter 18

Jerry thought that Gabe was already sitting as straight as a board, but when Phil asked him to tell them about Melia, he jerked his body up even more.

"Yaas'suh," he said in a quiver. "*Sh—She de gos'*."

"W—Who was she before she became a *ghost*?" Sarah asked. "Ghosts are real people first. Aren't they?" Her voice trailed off.

"She wuh r—real." Gabe worked at regaining his composure. "She wuh real awright."

"Will you tell us about her?" Phil repeated.

Gabe hesitated and started shaking his head from side to side. "Uh don' know. Uh cummin' too close tuh wuh muh granmudduh say don' do."

Gabe sat so still and quiet they thought for a moment he had fallen asleep. Finally, he said, "Reckon ent no haa'm tellin' oonuh youngins 'bout dat." He nodded his head up and down like it was on a spring before he said, "Way muh granmudduh tell it, Melia de Missus' kinfoke. She uh bute'ful lady wuh cum tuh de Brick House on Russell Crick fuh uh visit. Well, dis Melia she 'gaged tuh be marry w'en she cum tuh stay uh spell. Attuhw'ile she fall een lub wid sumboddy else. She write de fus' man dat

109

she lub dis odduh man now en' she gone marry him. De fus' man 'e cum tuh de islant, en' 'e beg huh don' marry noboddy else. 'E tell huh 'e rudduh see huh daid."

Lights from the campground made ghostly shadows in the trees behind Gabe.

Sarah held on to Marcy's hand, and now she squeezed it so tightly Marcy yelped in pain.

"Well," Gabe went on, "De night ub de widdin', de peoples all cum. De bittle spread. Melia Maum—dat huh serbant wuh cum wid huh tuh de islant—she upstairs wid Melia gittin' huh riddy fuh de widdin'." Gabe stopped; and, when he started up again, he seemed breathless. "'Bout dat time Melia heah sumboddy call huh name t'ru de winduh. Nat'ral, she go obuh en' look out tuh de daa'k. Dat w'en de man shoot huh daid. 'E dun clime up de big mossy oak 'en shoot huh t'ru de winduh. Den 'e kill hissef."

"OH, NO," Marcy said.

"How sad," Sarah added.

Gabe's voice took up the tremble again. "Melia wite dress stain wid blood. 'Fo' dat house bu'n, de winduh ledge she touch still got de blood stain.Uh see it wid muh own eyes. Don' mek no mine how many time it paint, it cum back. Yaas'suh. Dat house done bu'n, but fiah don' bodduh gos'. Melia still dere een dem bricks wid de vine climin' up 'um."

"Did you ever see or hear her?" Phil asked.

"Uh heah huh awright. She scream right outa de winduh." Gabe shut his eyes and shook his head from side to side as if his story was over.

"Gabe," Jerry dared to ask, "will you tell us what the plantation owner told your grandmother?"

As solemn as the night, Gabe whispered, "'E sho huh

weh 'e berry de silbuh." Then his voice picked up momentum. He seemed to hurry to get it all out before some unseen thing snatched the words right out of his mouth. "She say all de big bowl, de pitchuh, de fawk en' spoon en' de odduh pieces—all de big shiny silbuh een de house dey wrap een dc burlap bag en' pits een uh big baar'l. Dey puts tar een de crack tuh keeps de watuh out."

Sarah and Marcy clutched each other all the tighter. They couldn't believe what they were hearing.

Jerry whistled, and Phil whipped out his next question like an electric shock. "Did your grandmother tell anybody but you?"

"Uh de onliest one." Gabe held his hand out. "Uh 'bout dis high—" He studied it in the moonlight and lifted it slightly. "Dis high w'en she tuk me een de waggin back out tuh de Brick House. Ent noboddy libbin dere den. She say 'Gabe, case Uh die 'fo' sum ub de fambly cum back tuh claim dat silbuh, Uh gwine sho' oonuh weh it berry.'"

"Are you telling us," Jerry asked as the others hung on in disbelief, "that you know where silver was buried in the War Between the States?"

Gabe nodded. He seemed more relaxed now that he'd gotten it out. "But de t'ing is," he said slow and easy, "Uh cyan' sho' noboddy but de fambly weh dat at. En' dem buckruh, dey ent no fambly. Uh kin tell."

"I agree with you there," Jerry said. "Phil and I heard them talking, and they're crooks."

"They're crooks all right," Phil agreed. It was all coming together now.

To their disappointment, Gabe started up the trembling again. Jerry put his hand on the old man's knee in an effort to calm him.

"Wuh Uh gone tell oonuh now," he said, "Uh ent

nebbuh tole no libbin sole." He took a shaky breath. "Muh granmudduh say iffen Uh tell anyboddy outside de Brick House fambly weh dat silbuh at—she say **Melia gone git me.**"

"The GHOST?" Sarah asked.

Gabe nodded his head, and he couldn't seem to stop it from going up and down. "W'en she say dat, Uh heah Melia staa't screamin'. She scream en' scream. It so loud Uh 'bout ne'r tuh go crazy. Uh 'membuh Uh clime up een de waggin, en' de mules dey prancin' 'kase dey heah huh too. Dey tryin' tuh git de traces loose frum de tree weh muh granmudduh dun tie 'um. Uh cubbuhs muh head wid muh han', en' Uh promise obuh en' obuh Uh nebbuh gone sho' noboddy but de Brick House fambly. Attuhw'ile she stop screamin'."

A cloud slipped over the moon, throwing weird shadows over their faces and distorting their features.

"So the couple wants you to show them where the silver is buried?" asked Phil.

"LAWD HAB MUSSY." Gabe threw his hands up toward the heavens. "LAWD HAB MUSSY. Dat fuh sho wuh dey wonts wid me."

"How many people have you told about the silver, Gabe?" Jerry asked.

"Lawdy. Uh done tole hunduds ub foke 'bout de silbuh bein' berry. But Uh don' tell 'um 'bout Melia. De conjuh man 'e know Melia got sump'n' tuh do wid it, but 'e say 'e cyan' do nutt'n' wid no gos'."

"Nobody before has ever asked you to take them where the silver is buried?"

"Nawsuh, dey ent. Dey sho ent. Dey jes liss'n tuh muh story."

Jerry took Gabe by the arm. "Come on to bed," he said, "and don't you worry. If anybody tries to bother you tonight, they have to get by Phil and me first."

Gabe pulled himself up and stood for a moment as if to get steady. Then he moved toward his moss bed in the myrtle and to Eben.

Long after the girls had gone up to bed, clinging to each other against unseen ghosts, Phil and Jerry lay propped on their sleeping bags talking over their new information. Now that they had something to go on, they had to decide what to do about it.

Should they ask for help? If so, from whom? Would the police believe them? They had heard the maintenance man at the dock tell Gabe it was all in his head. But what proof did they have? A conversation they'd eavesdropped on at the couples' campsite. Another one as they hid in the shed. It would be their word against the couples'. They'd seen enough on TV to know lawyers like to say

113

young witnesses let their imaginations get the best of them.

Phil's parents? Phil thought of them sleeping just yards away in the camper. Guilt lay in his chest in a cold, hard lump. He hadn't lied to them. They *had* been listening to stories on the beach. But what would they think if they knew that he and Jerry at this moment kept guard for an old black man who feared for his life?

The sea breeze made walking sounds through the palmetto fronds. Why did the sound set Phil's heart beating faster? He leaned up to see Jerry. Was he asleep? Or was he thinking about Melia? He had told Phil all the old houses have ghosts. Was he thinking about that now?

If only the tide would take their troubles back out to sea and replace them with the carefree feeling of his first night on the beach. Things seemed much worse at night than in the daytime. Phil knew that. But, at the moment, daylight seemed a long time coming.

Chapter 19

True to what Phil thought, things did seem better in daylight. Gabe was up early, his moss bed under his arm and Eben by his side. He appeared to be over his fright of last evening and was eager to get to the creek to fish.

"If you'll wait, Gabe, I'll bring you down some breakfast," Phil promised, though not sure how he would manage to sneak something out.

"T'ank'e, but Uh gone stop by de IGA sto' en' git sump'n'."

"Be careful, Gabe," Jerry begged, "and watch out for those crooks."

"Uh stay close tuh de dock. Dey ent gone try nutt'n' long as Uh 'roun' peoples."

With the promise they would join him soon, they headed to the campsite.

"I wanted to ask him if he thought the spell was working," Jerry said, "but I didn't want to get him upset again."

"It was only yesterday we got the clothes you know." Phil spoke halfheartedly with a mumble of "If it works at all."

The girls were still asleep when the boys tackled the

pancakes and maple syrup Mr. Dunlap prepared for them.

Phil caught his breath when his dad said, "You fellows seem to be faring so well with that beach sleeping, I might even join you before we have to leave."

Jerry poked Phil under the table. "My dad tried it once, but he didn't last the night," he said.

Slipping their syrupy plates into the sudsy water of the small sink, they headed out. The girls were coming up from the bath house. "Will you wait for us to eat?" Marcy asked. "Sarah wants to show me Jeremy's Inlet. You can go with us."

Out of earshot, Jerry asked, "Was that Marcy's way of letting us know they wanted to talk to us before we went to watch out for Gabe?"

"Could be," Phil said, once again feeling bad about pulling the wool over his dad's eyes. "Say—" he said, "while they're getting ready, let's sneak up to the couple's site and see if they brought their boat back. If it's there, we don't have to worry about them getting to Gabe on the water."

Reliving the memory of the chase the day before, the boys made a silent trek up the beach and toward the sparsely scattered trees. "We should have checked on it last night instead of this morning in broad, open daylight," Jerry said.

Phil felt a shiver run over his body. He wouldn't have wanted to walk up the beach last night after hearing about Melia under any circumstances.

Cautiously they made their way to the clumps of myrtle and worked up far enough to see what they were after.

"The tent's up," Phil whispered, "but the car and boat are gone."

116

"Maybe they went to pull the boat in," Jerry whispered back. "They'd have to take the car to do that."

Mosquitoes had already set up a whine when they—with mixed feelings—slipped out of the myrtle thicket. If the tent hadn't still been there, they could hope the couple had given up and left the island. Now they didn't know what to think.

Back on the beach they spotted their sisters coming toward them.

"Are you really going to Jeremy's Inlet" Jerry asked, "or was that just some kind of message to wait for you?"

"Both," Marcy said. "Sarah wants me to see the inlet. She says it's really neat the way the tide swirls in and out."

"We need to see about Gabe. He went back to the dock," Phil said.

"Let's hurry on up to the inlet," Sarah said."It's not far, and then we'll go with you to the dock—even if it is smelly."

Phil looked at Jerry. His friend nodded. "Gabe'll be all right as long as he stays near the dock, and he said he would."

Phil still felt somewhat reluctant as they headed in the opposite direction from the dock. "I don't know about leaving Gabe unguarded. What we haven't told you girls is that the couple had their boat out on the water yesterday. We saw them up the creek toward Gabe's house."

"But we don't know that they still have it out," Jerry argued. "They could be pulling it in, and that's why the boat trailer's gone too."

Phil had seen Marcy's mouth drop open when he mentioned seeing the couple up the creek. Now she was full of questions.

117

They had no alternative but to fill in their sisters with the rest of the story—the trip to the conjurer's shack, a description of Gabe's house, the meal he prepared for them, and, most of all, their attempt to hide in the marsh.

"So that's why your shoes were such a mess!" Marcy exclaimed.

Caught up in the telling and listening to the events of the day before, they walked on—far beyond the campsite and along a deserted part of the beach. Before they knew it, they stood on the bank of Jeremy's Inlet.

"It's really hard to tell if the tide's coming in or going out just by looking," Sarah said. "Izzie's got a chart on her refrigerator that gives the times."

"You can tell by the water mark on the bank how far it usually comes up when it's in," Jerry said. "Of course if there's a storm it gets a lot higher."

"Like it did during that hurricane Izzie and your dad were talking about yesterday morning." Sarah pointed across the inlet. "That's the beach—Edingsville—where all those big houses got washed away."

"Yeah," Jerry said. "Now and then you hear of a fisherman or a hunter finding old pieces of china or something on the marsh side of the island."

"They used to have duels on that island too," Sarah said. "A man who was killed in one is buried in the Presbyterian Churchyard."

"The neatest thing, though," Jerry added, "is the island's got a ghost."

"Oh, no," Marcy said. "Please. *One* like Melia is enough."

"But this one's not like Melia," Jerry went on to explain. "Over a hundred years ago a ship wrecked during a bad storm, and a girl's body washed ashore. Nobody knew who she was, but they buried her on Edisto Island. When the moon's bright and the north wind dashes waves against the shore, they say you can see a beautiful woman dressed in white walking along the lonely beach. She comes back to look for her loved ones lost at sea."

"Awh, you should save that for tonight, Jerry," Phil teased.

"And, if anybody's brave enough to follow her," he added, "they see her disappear beneath the waves."

"Yeah, sure," Phil said. "We'll come back down here tonight and check her out."

"Oh," Sarah said, "it's only when the north wind whips up a gale that she appears."

"You believe it too, Sarah?" Phil asked.

"Now, Phil," his sister said, "don't tell me you believe Gabe's story but not Jerry's."

"I didn't say I believed the part about Melia."

"You sure acted like it last night."

"Last night was scary," Sarah said. "It gave me bad dreams."

"You should have tried sleeping on the beach after all that," Jerry said.

Phil looked at Jerry as he stooped to pick up a shell. His friend had felt the way he did last night after all.

"This inlet leads into Scott Creek. That's the same one the Indian Mound's on." He rubbed the velvety inner chamber of the big conch shell.

"Boy," Phil said. "These creeks really twist and wind around, don't they?"

All of a sudden the steady slosh of waves to their right was overpowered by the sound of a boat motor at full speed. The roar entered Phil's mind in a rumble of panic. He whipped around. What he saw fulfilled his worse fears. He tried to cry out to the others, but his words stuck in his throat. The boat with the couple shot down the ocean toward them.

Before they knew what was happening, the boat careened into the inlet, flinging salt water. The man cut the motor, and the boat rocked furiously.

"GET IN THE BOAT!" The big woman's words stung like a wasp.

Chapter 20

At her command Phil shifted his body for action. He was about to yell "Run!" when he saw her big hand reach into a bulging brown purse on the seat beside her. "Don't get any bright ideas!" she barked. "I'd hate to shoot kids in the back."

For an instance Phil couldn't breathe. His throat closed, trapping air in his chest in a painful lump. He didn't have to look at the others. He could feel their fright.

"You heard me." She yanked the purse up into her lap and set her mouth in an angry snarl. "All four of you, get in!"

"You takin' 'em all, Roxie?" The man wore a red bandana around his beak of a head.

"What do you think I'd do with the rest of 'em, numbskull? Drown 'em?" She stood up in the boat. Below her shorts, the muscles in her legs looked like a boxer's. "We sure can't let 'em go. They'd run and tell."

Jerry and Phil stepped into the waist-deep water of the inlet and started toward the boat. Phil had caught the edge of the boat to steady it when Sarah said, "We're not allowed in boats without life jackets. I don't see any."

"Or to go with strangers," Marcy added.

The man let out a nervous twitter. "I think we got us a couple of smart alecs," he said.

"If they know what's good for 'em, they'll shut up and follow orders." She emphasized her words with the motion of a muscular arm. "Help Red and her friend in the boat," she said to the boys, "and make it snappy."

Phil saw Marcy clamp her teeth down. She didn't like being called Red. He tried to stare her down to keep her quiet. Hadn't she seen the woman reach for her purse with the gun in it? Everybody knew you never argued with a person with a gun. Besides, her slitted eyes, too small for such a big face, gave her a mean look. He didn't doubt for a moment she would shoot them. When he thought of outrunning them, he hadn't counted on a loaded gun pointed at their backs.

The boat moved outward in the weakening wave action of the inlet as they strained to get in. Suddenly the bottom of the ocean dropped away without warning, and they clung onto the side for dear life. Phil managed to heave himself in first. With Jerry pushing and Phil pulling, they finally tumbled the girls in and Jerry followed.

Like half-drowned rats they scurried to find a place to hold on before the man jerked back the throttle, lurching the boat into action.

Suddenly a heavy crunching sound came from underneath. The motor groaned, sputtered, and nearly stopped.

"You dimwit!" Roxie yelled. "I thought you knew how to run a boat. You're tearing up the propeller in the shells on the bottom."

Momentarily they were enveloped in a whitish smoke and the smell of gasoline.

Another lurch threw them forward as the propeller churned into a second mound of shells and mud. Then in a streak they shot out of the inlet and onto the Atlantic Ocean, leaving a trail of tumbling white foam.

Phil's feelings sloshed about inside him. He didn't know whether the chatter of his teeth was from fear or chill. But one thing was perfectly clear: THEY WERE BEING KIDNAPPED!

"Where are you taking us?" Marcy called out. Her voice sounded so strange in the vibration of the speeding boat and wind, Phil looked to be sure it was his sister. She was pulling at the strands of hair being flung into her mouth.

"Shut your trap, Red, or you'll be shark bait!" The big woman sat in the bow facing them. Wind parted her black and yellow hair this way and that as the boat swerved in the waves.

Phil stared at Marcy again. She'd really better keep quiet. He wouldn't put it past this woman to throw them all overboard. Desperate people did things without thinking. He could feel the water moving under the boat just inches from his feet. The thought of a shark, like a shadowy missile shooting under water, terrified him.

Their wet clothing clung to their bodies. Spray peppered their arms and spewed in their faces. Sarah and Marcy slid down as far as they could in the boat, their arms wrapped tight across their chests.

On they raced at a maddening speed. The bow of the boat leaped from the water with each wave and landed with a jarring smack. With each smack, waves of fear washed over them. Phil could see it reflected in the others' faces.

Suddenly the front of the boat reared up so high they couldn't see in front of them. All in a moment the man cut the power, slamming into the shore with such force it almost catapulted them from the boat.

When the shock of the sudden stop waned, they spied a boat with two fishermen pulling in their lines. Marcy jumped up and yelled, "HELP! WE'RE BEING KID-NAPPED!"

As if her cry had been synchronized with the roar of the fishermen's boat taking off, the sound drowned out her voice.

"KIDNAPPED?" The man they'd heard Roxie call Hugh jumped up and flailed his arms. "You never said nothin' 'bout no kidnappin'. I ain't havin' nothin' to do with no kidnappin'. They put you in the 'lectric chair for that. See if your precious Biff can help you then."

"Oh, shut up your whinin'. We're just dumpin' 'em over here until we can finish up our business with the old man." To her cargo she said, "Get out!"

Chapter 21

Feeling helpless, the four did as they were told and climbed out of the boat onto the deserted, almost treeless shore. Hugh rammed the motor in reverse, then thrust it forward, jerking Roxie's head back, and they were off. Their voices, pitted against each other, drifted back across the water.

"From what they said, they're going after Gabe." Dejection showed in Phil's voice. "We're in a mess now. We should have gone on to the dock in the first place."

"It's not our fault that they took us captive," Marcy blurted out.

"I didn't say it was your fault we were kidnapped, but it would have been if they'd thrown us overboard. They had a gun you know. I can't believe you kept on taunting them."

"I wasn't taunting them. That woman was making me mad calling me Red."

"Do you know where we are?" Phil asked Jerry.

"It must be Botany Bay Island by the looks of these conchs, but I don't recognize this part." He started around the bend.

"At least we are away from those awful people." Sarah

126

hugged herself and shivered. "I was scared out of my wits in that boat."

"Don't think I wasn't," Marcy said. "Roxie, or whatever her name was, is one mean woman."

"This is Botany Bay all right," Jerry called back. "That's Frampton's Inlet down that way. The only thing is that inlet is a lot wider than Jeremy's. I don't think we can cross it to get back."

"I thought you knew every nook and cranny of Edisto Beach," Phil reminded him.

"I know these islands have all sorts of sandbars and shallows around them. They don't show until low tide, and by the looks of things that won't be until near dark."

"Great. Just great," Phil said. "Whatever they're going to do to Gabe will be done by then. We really let him down."

"But we didn't have any idea they wanted *us*—not without him anyway," Jerry defended their actions.

"So we're stranded," Marcy said.

"At least until the tide goes down. Even then, if the water's still over our heads. It's too dangerous to try to swim an inlet. Sometimes the current in waist-deep water will pull you out."

"Gee, thanks for all your information, Jerry." Marcy plopped down on the beach.

"And," Jerry went on, "you never can tell when a squall will come off the Atlantic. That's one reason this island looks so barren with the driftwood and all. It really takes a beating from the ocean."

"Maybe we can get back by land over that way." Phil pointed behind them.

"Nope. That's all marshland—big marshland. In front of us is the Atlantic Ocean."

"Well, we all know that, Jerry," Sarah said.

"What he's telling us," Phil threw up his hands, "is that we're on an island, completely cut off—except by boat. That couple knew exactly what they were doing when they dumped us here."

"There is one hope," Jerry told them. "The man who rides the people over to pick up shells may be bringing a load over, and we could get him to take us back."

Faces were showing interest when he added, "But, what I can't understand is that nobody else is on the island now. Like we explained earlier, he brings a load, drops them, and goes back for another. You can go back on any of his return trips or just tell him when to come for you. Of course, he doesn't go down to Edisto Beach. He goes up the inlet, but we could call from there."

"So exactly what is it you're saying?" Phil asked.

"That he's probably playing golf today. He likes golf."

"Super," Phil said.

"Look at this shell," Marcy said. "It's humongous!"

"There's no need to waste time gathering them up," Jerry said. "If we walk back—and that's a long, long way—you won't be able to take them. We always take along plastic bags when we collect shells."

"So," Marcy said sarcastically, "what do you suggest I do with my time while I'm here? Just work at getting blistered. Or, maybe I could make a picnic lunch and invite all of you over."

Jerry and Sarah looked at Marcy in bewilderment.

"Cut it out, Marcy," her brother said. "Picking a fight won't help. We've all got to work together. At least Mom and Dad won't be worried about us—until much later anyway. Dad said they were riding into Walterboro to-day."

"And Izzie will think we're with you, so she won't be worried either," Sarah said.

"But you want to know something else?" Marcy asked. "Since nobody will be worried, they won't even know we're missing."

"Oh, no," Sarah groaned. "I hadn't thought of that." She plopped down by Marcy. "Well, there's not a thing we can do about it."

"Jerry was right about one thing." Marcy pulled herself up to stare down at a huge piece of wood. "This driftwood belongs in a Dracula movie."

Sarah joined her, and they strolled around the island, picking up a shell here and there in spite of Jerry's saying they couldn't carry them back. Soon they lost sight of the boys.

Along the shore, foam from the surf had caught up in driftwood. Fragile bubbles made by the breeze clung on for survival. That's what she felt like, Marcy decided. A fragile bubble—all empty inside. And they'd had such fun—until today.

A gasp from Sarah stopped her short. "Look!" she said.

A piece of driftwood stuck up on a barren dune like a growing tree. Someone had hung broken conchs on the branches. It was the eeriest sight Marcy had ever seen. Suddenly the place was a Western desert in a cowboy movie, and a grave site marked with a cross had just been discovered. "Let's show it to the boys," she said, somehow feeling the need of their company.

They found them leaning over a pile of shells and broken pieces of driftwood. "I tell you it won't work," Phil was saying. "You need flint to start a fire."

They all heard the boat motor at the same time. At

129

first the same fear gripped them: the couple was returning. But then they caught sight of a boat with fun-filled people. Laughter drifted over.

In a moment the four of them were shouting, jumping up and down, and screaming "Help!" Phil jerked off his shirt, stuck it on a piece of driftwood, and waved it frantically back and forth.

The pleasure seekers waved back in fun and sped on down toward Edisto Beach. Hope gone, they watched until the sound faded and the boat became a black dot on the horizon.

"They thought we were just waving at them," Jerry said, the punch gone from his voice. Then he dropped his head back and looked straight up. "Good grief," he said, "turkey buzzards."

"The ones that eat dead things!" Sarah grabbed Marcy and held on.

"Well, I don't think they're after us," Phil consoled. "At least not yet."

"Look." Jerry pointed to the shrimp boats silhouetted against the horizon. "They're going in early. They must be expecting bad weather."

"Oh, I hope not," Marcy complained. "I'm just halfway getting rid of this awful smell of wet clothes."

Overhead, gulls gave a laughing call and terns swooped and cried. A wind kicked up, turning the north sky dark and filling their mouths with salt and sand.

All of a sudden gloom enveloped them. "It's like we're c—cut off from the world." Nobody tried to contradict Sarah. She felt near tears.

"I know what we can do." Proud of her idea, Marcy grabbed a conch in each hand. "Let's clear a space and write HELP! in big letters with these shells."

"It would take a helicopter to see it," Phil said, but he'd already begun to pick up the biggest ones near him.

By the time they put in the exclamation mark, the sea had become a seething mass. Dark clouds gathered and scudded across the sky. Wind gusted. Lightning flashed in a jagged white streak. Suddenly the ocean and sky became one in a drenching downpour.

"Follow me!" Jerry raced toward the inlet.

Stumbling on shells and straining to see a step ahead, they trailed the moving form. Another flash of lightning in jagged daggers. A boom of thunder.

After what seemed forever, they crouched together in a sandy ravine on the inlet. What Marcy had learned in school came back to her: always get to the lowest spot when lightning catches you in an open space. She was glad Jerry remembered. They would have been lightning rods on the shore.

How long they stayed huddled in the storm they didn't know. Watches did no good in the blinding rain. Marcy was sure it was hours. Then, just like somebody had turned off a water faucet, the rain stopped. Thin streamers of white clouds floated high above the fading gray of the sky.

In the next moment Jerry yelled out. They all jumped. Was it a cry of pain or pleasure? They couldn't tell until they saw where he was pointing.

Chapter 22

Jerry pointed up Frampton's Inlet. While the storm raged, the tide had gone out. A sandbar they could walk across lay inches beneath the moving water.

Dripping wet from the storm, they rushed toward it, shouting in happiness.

"Hold on!" Jerry cautioned. "We can't be too careful, even when the tide's down. Remember those teachers? They died on the creek, *not* the ocean. And it took days for one body to wash up."

"We get it, Jerry," Marcy said. "You don't have to say any more."

Spirits dampened by Jerry's sober remarks, they stepped cautiously across a narrow trench of sea water and onto the sandbar. Jerry insisted they stay together so they could point out gullies holding deeper water and soft spots with sucking sand. In some places the water came up to their knees.

"The way I see it—" Jerry looked at his waterproof watch. "It's going to take about an hour and a half, maybe two, to walk back."

"You've got to be kidding," Phil said in disbelief.

"We'll be dead by then," Marcy remarked, and Sarah

looked as if the tears were too close to the surface to make a sound.

Once across the inlet, they breathed easier. On they trekked. The wind, like an open hand, pushed at their backs with every step.

"At least, Marcy, the storm kept you and Phil from getting blistered," Sarah said.

Marcy gave her a weak smile. "My Grandmother Bhaer would like you, Sarah. She's always telling me to be an optimist."

Phil started to make a comment, but he thought better of it. Now was no time to try to have the last word with Marcy. He had said earlier that bickering would get them nowhere. Now he needed to practice what he preached, as his dad liked to say. Besides, they needed to save their energy. The day was long from over.

Shorebirds high-stepped along in front of them and cocked their heads as if listening. Then, with a jerk of their thin legs, they took off in a chase of the retreating tide. Another big bird spread its wings in flight over the choppy waves.

"If we could only fly—" Sarah mused.

"Are you sure there's no way we can contact anybody on this island either, Jerry?" Phil asked.

"Nope. Noboby lives on it. It's all marshland and creeks back that way."

"These shells are killing my feet, even through my shoes," Sarah complained.

"Couldn't we stop and rest, at least for a little while?" asked Marcy. "My legs are dead."

"So are mine," Jerry answered, "but it's already going to be dark before we get back. Look." He pointed to the thin stretch of light between the ocean and the sky. "We need to hurry."

Heavy with dampness, they plodded on—each lost in his and her own thoughts. Were the others thinking of Gabe too? Phil wondered. What if the couple did overtake him? And what would they do with him if he refused to show them where the silver was buried? Would he try to explain to them about Melia?

A dark mood had settled over them when Sarah asked, "Shouldn't we be at Jeremy's Inlet soon?" She looked down at the long curling strand of black seaweed lying on the sand like a thick snake.

"Edingsville is a long island," Jerry said.

"EDINGSVILLE?" Marcy screamed. "Do you mean we're on the island where the girl walks the beach looking for the others lost at sea?"

"Where did you think we were, Marcy?" her brother asked. "You know we're not at Edisto yet?"

At that moment all traces of light slipped away, leaving a night sky not yet studded with stars and a ghostly white moon hanging over the ocean.

"Jerry," Marcy dared to ask, "is the wind coming from the north?"

"Yeah. I'd say north or northeast. Why?"

"Didn't you say that was when the girl gets up out of her grave and does her walking?"

"Marcy, *please*." Sarah begged. "Let's don't talk about it."

Marcy respected her friend's request, but she couldn't shake the feeling the girl would be coming over the dune at any moment, her white dress blowing in the wind. On their left the sea rushed angrily toward them. Was it that way the night she drowned? Like cold fingertips, a shiver started at the nape of her neck and ran down her back. In her fright she reached out and grabbed Sarah's arm.

Sarah let out a piercing shriek. Jerry and Phil swung around in a wild frenzy. "WHAT THE—!" Jerry hollered.

"Marcy scared the daylights out of me," Sarah said. "I—I was thinking about the man killed in the duel on this island."

"Well, why don't you both just stop thinking?" Phil asked. "Carrying on like this isn't helping anything."

Time dragged until they finally reached the spot where they had been taken captive. All traces of daylight had disappeared. A cold yellow moon contrasted with the dark sky.

Memories of their throats tight with fear seemed to fall back upon them. Thankful the tide was down, they edged along the sloping bank of Jeremy's Inlet and slipped into the waist-deep water.

"We need to hold hands." Jerry reached out and grabbed Marcy's hand. "Get between the girls," he called to Phil. "In case one of us gets in the deepest part, the others can pull them along. This inlet might be narrower; but it's deeper, and the tide's lots stronger."

With the sound of the ocean rushing in their ears, they worked their soggy shoes against the swift current in a human chain. The short distance to the other side seemed to take forever. Finally, they arrived and helped each other onto the shore.

Brisk breezes chilled their bodies under wet clothing. A fine mist from the sea hung in the air like spider webs.

"I—I'm cold." Sarah's teeth chattered.

"Me too," Marcy said. "Maybe if we ran awhile, it would warm us up."

They started out in a slow jog, taking care to stay on the damp sand for easier running and to watch out for ridges of sharp shells glistening in the moonlight.

Breaths came in jagged huffs and groans. The wind had lessened and no longer pushed them along. Gradually, they slowed until just walking became a chore.

"I'm dying of thirst," Jerry said, and Phil added, "Join the party."

"At least we've got moonlight." Sarah gazed at the egg-shaped moon halfway up the sky.

"Yeah," Marcy agreed. "And it's almost full. Just a slender wedge on one side is missing."

Nobody seemed to have the urge to keep the conversation going. Phil wondered if the others were also thinking about Gabe. If only they would find him and Eben under the myrtles when they reached the campground. If they didn't, how would they know where to look for him? And worst of all, would they be too late?

As if Jerry read Phil's mind, he said, "I hope Gabe will be in the hiding place we made for him, and—" His voice trailed off, but his sentence needed no ending. They were all of one mind.

At last the campground came into view. In spite of the ghostly gleam cast by the lights, they were a welcome sight.

Fear of passing close to the couple's site and the urgency of seeking Gabe in the myrtles gave them a boost of energy. They picked up a fast run-walk toward the secret hideout.

Even before they reached the spot, Phil knew something was wrong, dreadfully wrong.

Straining to see in the dark bushes, they had their worse fears confirmed. Eben lay curled on the moss sleeping bag. But Gabe was nowhere in sight.

Chapter 23

The four stood staring helplessly on the crest of the dune. "Something's happened to Gabe," Phil said. "I know it has."

"You're right," Jerry agreed. "Eben wouldn't be here without him. They go everywhere together."

"Maybe he's in the bath house." Sarah's breath came in burning bursts.

Caught up in Sarah's comment, they hurried down the beach in a follow-the-leader pattern and cut up over the dune toward the bath house. The bright lights of that area lifted their spirits slightly, only to squash them. No Gabe.

They pulled their weary bodies back over the dune and up the beach toward their campsite. The Dunlaps' car was gone. Their camper was dark. Where were their parents? Were they out looking for them?

On the screened enclosure Phil fumbled for the lamp and the camper key stored beneath it.

"Now what?" Marcy asked as he fiddled with the key in the lock.

"We've got to get to a telephone," Phil answered. He swung the door aside and flipped on lights. Then he stopped in his tracks and looked at Jerry. "We don't have any choice now but to call the police. If Gabe was free, he would be with Eben."

"If Dad were here—"

"Well, he isn't, Marcy," Phil shot back. "And anyway, these people are a lot more dangerous than we thought. It's a job for the police."

"Okay, Phil," Jerry consented. "I guess you're right. We've done all we can do on our own."

"There's a pay phone outside the park office building," Marcy said.

"I know," Phil replied, "but we had to come get money to call."

"I can't understand what's happened to Mom and Dad." Marcy scouted the refrigerator door for a note. She looked over the sink, the table. Nothing. "They'd never be away this long without leaving a note or phoning—"

"We don't have a phone. Remember?" Phil reminded her.

"Let's go to Izzie's," Sarah suggested. "Maybe they called her."

"As soon as we notify the police that Gabe's missing," Phil said. "And, Marcy, leave Dad and Mom a note that we'll be at Izzie's."

"Get a flashlight," Jerry said, "so we can see how to dial."

Marcy propped the note to her parents over the sink. "What about the police number?" she asked.

"It's on the bulletin board," Jerry said, "but bring your pencil and paper so we can copy it."

The camper locked and the outside lamp burning, they hurried to the bulletin board near the office for the number and on to the phone. The building was closed up tight.

"I'll dial, Jerry, and you talk," Phil said.

The three stood listening in as Jerry identified himself and told the problem. "I know he's an old man who tells stories," he said into the phone, "but I tell you he's in trouble. His dog is in the myrtle bushes, and he's missing. My sister, my two friends, and I have just walked all the way back from Botany Bay Island where this couple dumped us after they kidnapped us and—" . . .

"I'm calling you from the campground phone. . . . Yes, we have parents, but we don't know where my friends' parents are, and my grandmother doesn't know about this. . . . Sir, if you don't believe me, you're going to be sorry when Gabe's dead." Jerry's voice showed frustration. . . .

"Will you please just station an officer at the Dawhoo Bridge so the man and woman can't get off the island. . . . Just a minute, Sir." He turned to the three circled around him. "He says the draw bridge is caught in the up position, and nobody can get on or off the island."

"Then that explains why Mom and Dad aren't back!" Marcy exclaimed.

"But, Sir," Jerry continued, "if you'll just put an officer there, he could catch them *trying* to get away. The woman is big with funny yellow hair, and the man is weaselly. . . . All right. I'll hold on."

Jerry turned to his friends again and cupped his hand over the receiver. "He's putting the officer in charge on the phone. I can hear him. He's telling him some kid says a weird couple has old Gabe."

"Yes, Sir. Yes, Sir," Jerry said into the phone. "They're trying to make him tell them where some silver was buried during the War Between the States. They tried to take him from his house on Big Bay Creek. . . . You do know where that is? . . . You do? . . . And, Sir, be careful. They've got a gun. . . . We'll be at my grandmother's— Izzie Curry. Her house is on Palmetto Boulevard, and it's called High Tide. . . . 868-9939. And PLEASE HURRY."

"Whew!" Jerry hung up the phone and let out his breath in a stream of air. "I didn't think he was going to do anything about it at first. He started telling me that Gabe had always told his old stories to anybody who would listen and that people didn't pay him any mind."

"But he'll look for him?" Phil asked.

"Said he'd get right on it and wanted to know where he could reach us if he needed us. I gave him Izzie's number so let's head on there."

"Shouldn't we go on the street side?" Phil asked. "You said we can't take a flashlight on the beach on account of the turtles."

Jerry nodded. The girls agreed they'd had enough beach walking, and they were off again.

"Ugh!" Marcy groaned when they were headed down the sidewalk. "I feel like I'm coated with slime."

"Me too," Sarah said.

Steps ahead of them their brothers moved like two shadows. Tired, hungry, and dirty, they plodded toward High Tide.

The slam of the screened door brought a call from Izzie at the bridge table. "It's about time you kids showed up." Her back was to them.

This was not the place to start in with their story, Jerry decided. "It doesn't seem as dark outside," he said, trying his best not to let his voice show his weariness, "when you haven't been in where it's lighted."

"That's true, Izzie," a friend said in a fun-filled voice.

"Jerry's exactly right. It doesn't. I bid *three no trump*."

"Oh, by the way, Marcy and Phil—" Izzie spoke over her shoulder. "Your parents heard the bridge into the island was out of order so they decided to stay in Walterboro overnight. You kids are to sleep here. Jerry and Sarah will show you around." She turned then to look at them. "Good heavens!" she cried. "You look like drowned rats."

"We'll get baths," Jerry said. "But first is there something we can eat and drink?"

"Hot dogs—all the way—in the refrigerator. Loosen the Saran wrap and stick them in the microwave. And there's chips and milk."

"And," Izzie's cheery-voiced bridge partner added, "you're in luck. I brought over a pan of brownies after I found out about the visitors."

From the kitchen they heard a voice say, "My son left his car on the riverbank and took a boat over. Several of the islanders are providing transportation. The Dunlaps probably didn't know that."

"Now, let me review the bidding," another player said. "A *pass, two clubs, two spades*. Right? Okay—*five clubs*."

Too tired to talk, and caught in a jumble of thoughts and worries, they ate quietly. Sarah and Marcy left the boys at the table still devouring brownies and milk to drag themselves off for baths.

"Oh, no," Marcy groaned. "Why didn't I pick up some clothes while we were in the camper?"

"Don't worry," Sarah assured her, "I'll find something that'll fit you."

"Whatever it is," Marcy said, "I'll sleep in it too."

"I have a feeling it won't be long before the four of us

will be dead to the world," Sarah said.

Sarah's prediction wasn't far from wrong. Fresh from their baths, they plopped on the screened porch to watch television. Without saying so, each knew thoughts of Gabe pricked at the others' minds like splinters.

Izzie's and her friends' laughter and bridge jargon mingled with the whooshing of waves and a rerun of *Family Matters*, lulling their tired bodies. Suddenly a knock at the street side jerked them into reality.

"Law me, Izzie," a voice said. "There's a police officer at your door."

Chapter 24

"Officer—" Izzie stood with her hands on her slender hips. "I haven't the foggiest idea what you're talking about. You mean you want the children?"

The three bridge partners sat as if somebody had thrown them into positions in a game of freeze tag. Mouths hung open. Cards poised in midair, and eyes darted from Izzie to the officer to the children crowded in the doorway.

"We were going to tell you, Izzie," Jerry said, "when you got through with your bridge game."

"TELL ME WHAT, FOR PETE'S SAKE?"

"It's a long story," Phil offered.

"If you don't mind, Ma'am," the officer said, "suffice it to say for now that the children have been trying to rescue old Gabe—"

"Rescue Gabe? Where is he, for heaven's sake?"

"Is he all right?" Phil and Jerry cried at the same time.

"He was here yesterday," Izzie blurted out before the officer had time to answer.

"Yes, Ma'am," the officer went on. "But today he was taken captive—"

"TAKEN CAPTIVE?" Izzie repeated. Behind her,

bridge players gasped.

"Ah, yes, Ma'am—by a couple we've just apprehended, and if you don't mind, I'd like to take the children down to identify them."

Izzie opened her mouth as if to speak, but Jerry beat her to it with a quick "Where's Gabe?"

"At the police station."

"Does he know you're not putting him in jail?" Jerry asked. "He's afraid of jails."

The officer was nodding even before Jerry finished. "He's fine—just worried about you kids. Said the couple left you on Botany Bay Island."

"LEFT YOU ON BOTANY BAY ISLAND?" Izzie's voice reached a high pitch. "YOU MEAN TO TELL ME—" She looked at Jerry and then the others.

"It's okay, Izzie." Jerry had never seen his grandmother so upset. "We'll tell you all about it when we get back."

"Well," a club member said as they headed out, "I, for one, am not budging from this house until they get back."

. . . . .

"That blonde-headed woman is as stirred up as a hornet's nest," the officer said as they drove toward the police station.

Sarah leaned toward Marcy in the back seat. "I don't want to see her again," she said.

"She can't bother us now," Jerry said from the seat next to her.

"That's right, young man. She's behind bars, right where she ought to be. The chief was having their records checked when I left to come for you."

"Where'd you find them?" Phil asked.

"Out at the Brick House ruins. They had the old man at gunpoint trying to make him identify the tree where the silver was buried."

"Did he tell them?" Jerry asked.

"When we got there, Gabe was hollering 'HALLELU-JAH! I CAN'T 'MEMBER DE TREE. I TELL DE TRUFE. I TELL DE TRUFE.'"

"That's good," Marcy explained to the officer, "because he was afraid a ghost would get him if he ever told where that silver was buried."

"That sounds like Gabe." The officer pulled into the station before he added, "Well, he's safe now—thanks to you kids."

"There's the old green car!" Sarah said.

"Old is right," the officer said. "I had the pleasure of driving it back from the Brick House."

On seeing Gabe sitting on a bench near the chief's desk, the four momentarily forgot their fear of facing their kidnappers. They ran to Gabe with hugs.

"Where were you when the couple got you, Gabe?" Jerry asked.

"Uh dodge 'um all day 'tell mos' daa'k w'en Uh wawk up tuh de campgroun' tuh look fuh oonuh. Uh pits muh bed een de myrtle, en' den Uh wawks tuh de bath house. Eben 'e folluh me. Dat w'en dey grab me."

"That explains why we found Eben on the moss bed in the myrtles," Marcy said.

Gabe's face brightened. "Uh figguh Eben go dere." Yaas'suh. De buckruh s'prised tuh see me. Dey dun gib up on me 'tell de biddy man, 'e run slap dab eentuh me, en' 'e holluh tuh de 'ooman. Dey pull out de gun en' tell me no youngins gone hep me now 'kase dey dun dump 'em on de shell islant."

145

"Here comes the report," the chief called. His assistant moved to the computer. "Well, I'll be!" he said. "WOULD YOU LOOK AT THAT!" He began to read aloud:

> Bulletin out for female, known as Roxie—buxom blonde, last seen dressed in sequinned blouse and driving green Studebaker; male, known as Hugh—small, wiry, wearing Western garb; both in thirties; believed to be wanted in silver theft ring along coasts of Georgia and South Carolina.

"All we need now," the chief said, "is an identification that these are the people who kidnapped you kids."

Phil and Jerry struck out down the corridor behind the officer. Reluctantly the girls followed.

The second they were in sight of the cells, Hugh started yelling, "Listen to me. Listen to me."

Phil thought he looked for all the world like some exotic bird with his nose sticking through the bars.

From the adjoining cell, Roxie screeched, "You'd better shut your trap if you know what's good for you!"

"Ask the kids." The man stuck his boney hand through the bars. "They can tell you I said I wasn't havin' nothin' to do with no kidnappin'. I didn't know she was plannin' nothin' like that. Ask the kids."

"Calm down. Both of you," the officer said. "You'll have your day in court, and we'll get statements from the children." He turned to them. "Well, I guess Hugh took care of the identification for us. But, you do agree these are the people who abducted you?"

Thankful the bars were between them and Roxie, Jerry said, "Yes, Sir. That's them all right." The others nodded.

When the children started to leave, Gabe got up. "Uh

146

be gwine wid de chillun," he said.

"Gabe," Jerry touched his arm. "We've got to stay at Izzie's tonight. Phil's parents aren't home. Maybe you can stay here, and we'll come back in the morning."

Gabe's eyes grew large. The officer put his hand on his shoulder. "Tell you what," he said, "why don't we go down and bring your dog up to be with you. I'm holding duty tonight, and you can sleep on the cot in the back room."

"Anyway," the chief said, "I'm on my way home as soon as you fetch your dog, and I'll need you in the morning to fill out my forms." He looked to the group for their support. "And, I'll give you a good breakfast."

"Sounds good to me, Gabe," Jerry said, and the others agreed.

When the officer returned them to Izzie's, the bridge group was waiting, anxiously—all ears. As quickly as he could, Jerry recapped the happenings of the last few days, careful to leave out about the conjure man.

The ladies sat wild eyed. "You mean you walked all the way from Botany Bay Island?" the one who made the brownies asked.

"And we're dead," Sarah said, her appearance bearing out her words.

"It's been the longest day of my life," Marcy declared.

With Izzie's promise to her friends that they would learn everything she did at a later date, she shooed the children off to bed.

Before sleep overshadowed all the unanswered questions, Phil's mind clung to one in particular: *what about the conjure man and his spell now?*

147

Chapter 25

At Izzie's breakfast table, they picked up the conversation of the night before.

"I just want Dad to be able to talk with Gabe," Phil said between mouthfuls of Cheerios.

"Tell you what—" Izzie said, still not able to take it all in. "When your parents called yesterday, I asked them down for a shrimp boil tonight. Why don't you invite Gabe?"

"We'd better hurry and get to him," Jerry said, "before he goes back up the creek."

Still looking a bit puzzled by it all, Izzie answered a phone call from a bridge partner. With a high sign, the four hurried out and toward the police station to see Gabe.

To their surprise, the couple had already been escorted to Beaufort to answer an earlier charge. The chief was winding up his paper work with Gabe.

"You fellows were right," he said. "I just got off the phone with the officer who faxed the information last night. Seems the leader of this silver theft ring—somebody called Biff—came up with the idea of finding the old buried silver. He'd send a scout out to try to locate the silver, a second group—in this case our strange couple—to mark the spot, and a third party to dig it up."

"Since nobody could live at the ruins of the Brick House," Jerry said, "they probably thought that would be a good choice."

"Exactly. They're clever all right." He turned to Gabe. "I think our partner here is going to be more selective about who he tells his stories to from now on."

"Dat right." Gabe grinned. "Uh sho is."

The chief rose in his efficient way. "Well, thanks to you—" He waved his hand over the group. "This is one ring that's all washed up."

We're just glad you got there in time to save Gabe," Jerry said.

"So are we." The chief offered his hand to Gabe. "So, it's back to fishing as usual, eh, Gabe?" He was off to the business of the day.

"Gabe," Sarah asked, "are you going home now?"

"Dat wuh Uh gone do." He nodded. "Me en' Eben, we gwine home."

"Izzie wants you to come to dinner at High Tide around sundown," Jerry said. "Phil's dad wants to meet you. All the Dunlaps will be there."

Gabe hesitated until Phil said, "Will you come, Gabe? Tonight's our last night on the island."

"Uh do dat," he said, nodding. "Uh sho do dat."

"By the way, Gabe," Phil asked as they started to part, "Have you seen the conjure man?"

"Uh gone go by 'is house on de way home en' tells 'im 'bout t'ing'."

. . . . .

With the bridge repaired, the Dunlaps arrived back on the island to reports they found hard to believe. Mrs. Dunlap grabbed Marcy and Phil and lavished on them her famous butterfly kisses—her eyelashes batting against their cheeks. "If I had known what was happening," she kept repeating, "I would have been out of my mind."

The rest of the day was taken up in explaining to the adults how they had gotten involved with the weird couple and their plot to force Gabe to show them where the silver was buried. They even ventured so far as to tell them about the conjure man.

"I'm very much interested in that," Mr. Dunlap said. "Superstition was a vital part of the culture brought over with the slaves."

When they recounted Gabe's fear of Melia, Izzie said, "That's really *Amelia*. She's in Mrs. Graydon's book—a lovely girl killed by a broken-hearted lover."

"There's something so sad about a person returning to the place where life was unfulfilled for them," Mrs. Dunlap said.

"Mom," Phil said, "you sound as if you believe in ghosts."

Before she could respond, her husband said, "Your mother's an eternal romantic. That's another reason I married her."

. . . . .

When Gabe arrived at Izzie's, he was so spruced up they hardly recognized him. Even Eben looked as if he'd had a scrub down.

The small home appeared to be bursting at the seams as everybody answered Izzie's call to take food to the picnic table on the deck.

"Oh, no!" Marcy cringed at the platter of shrimp. "They've still got shells on them and little dangly feet."

Izzie laughed. "That's the only way to eat shrimp at the beach."

"Be glad they don't have the heads still on them," Jerry said.

"As the saying goes," Izzie added, "no shell 'em, no eat 'em. Besides, Gabe catches the very best." She gave him a big smile.

Izzie stuck a bean salad for the table in Sarah's hand and French bread in Marcy's. "Here, detectives," she said to the boys, "you're in charge of putting ice in glasses and finding out what people want to drink."

The mood of the evening was jovial. Marcy managed to peel her shrimp and slip the shells under the edge of her plate so she wouldn't have to look at them while she ate. Pleasant sounds drifted up from walkers along the beach; waves rolled against the shore. Only Mrs. Dunlap's occasional "If you'd only told us!" rubbed against the pure contentment of the evening.

Finally her husband said, "I agree with you, Honey. It worries me to think the children might have been harmed. However, the officer assured me these kinds of people are up on ways to get around the law. If they hadn't been caught red-handed—thanks to the kids—they would most likely have gone scot-free to some other place to do the same thing."

"Yes," his wife answered, "but hauling the children off in that boat—at gunpoint—"

"That was pretty scary," Phil said. "That is, to all of us except Marcy. She almost got us fed to the sharks."

"Marcy?" her mother looked at her in disbelief.

"Phil knows I was scared." She glared at her brother. "But that Roxie woman made me mad calling me *Red*."

"I think you have beautiful hair," Izzie said. "I wish mine was that color."

"You could make yours that way," Sarah suggested.

"Oh, I don't have the complexion for it," she responded, "it wouldn't look right on me."

"Gabe," Phil said, "I still don't see how you kept from telling them where the silver was buried with a gun at your head. The officer said you couldn't remember. Was that true, or were you just saying that?"

"It de trufe awright. Seem lak dey wuz onliest one big oak w'en muh granmudduh show it tuh me. Now dey trees all up en' down dat crick. How Uh gone know wich one?"

"Sounds like the police came in the knick of time." Mr. Dunlap said.

"Dey did. Dey sho did. T'anks tuh muh fr'en' heah." Gabe gave a low chuckle. "Gess dat tredjuh gone stay right weh it berry."

They were about to get up from the table when Phil remembered. "Gabe," he asked, "did you find the conjure man?"

"Uh sho did. 'E said 'is wife fount de onduhclo'es een de draw'r, en' she t'ink dat bra b'long tuh 'is gullfr'en'. She t'ro it en' de odduh piece een de fiah en' bu'n 'em up 'fo' 'e ebbuh got tuh wu'k de magic."

Seeing Gabe so serious, the others tried to suppress their smiles.

With the adults settled inside around Gabe and Mr. Dunlap's recorder, the young people walked down on the beach.

"I hate you've got to leave so soon," Jerry said. "We

152

didn't even get to ride the waves or fish from the pier."

"But we did get to go to Botany Bay Island," Marcy said.

They laughed, and Sarah added, "But not the way we planned." She caught her breath. "You know what I just thought of? Those shells are still spelling out HELP! on that island."

"Oh, no!" Marcy groaned. "And it was my idea."

"Don't worry," Jerry said. "Somebody'll pick them up tomorrow. They were choice shells." And in the next breath, he asked, "Where will you go from here?"

"To a school on St. Helena Island—Penn, I think," Phil said.

"Ive been there," Jerry said. "It's near Beaufort. . . . But you better watch out. That's where Roxie said old Biff is. Remember?"

Phil gave a nervous laugh. "They should all be behind bars by now."

"Well, one thing's for sure," Marcy said. "It's no laughing matter. At least, not any time soon."

Remembering their experience, they turned back toward High Tide and hung over the deck rail looking at a sky filled with points of light.

"You know," Phil said, "it's kind of neat to know there really are buried treasures along this coast."

"Okay," Jerry said," whoever wants to find a buried treasure next summer, put it there." He stuck out his hand—palm up—and the others slapped their hands on to his.

The End

Glossary

aig - egg, eggs
attuh - after
ax - ask, asked
baar'l - barrel
bawn - born
behime - behind
berry - bury
bittle - food
'bliged - obliged
bodduh - bother
buckruh - white people/
    person
bu'n - burn
bute'ful - beautiful
cawdgrass - cordgrass
chillun - children
clo'es - clothes
conjuh - conjure
crick - creek
cubbuh - cover
cum'fuh - come for
cyah - care
cyan' - can't
daa'k - dark
daid - dead
dat - that
dayclean - daylight
de - the
den - then
dere - there
dere's - theirs, there is

dese - these
dey - they
dis - this
'e - he
eben - even
een - in
eentuh - into
en' - and
ent - is not, are not
en't'ing' - and other things
enty - is it not so
fawk - fork
feel han' - field hand
fiah - fire
figguh - figure
'fo' - before
foke - folk
folluh - follow
fr'en' - friend, friends
frum - from
fuh - for
fus' - first
Gawd - God
gos' - ghost
granmudduh - grandmother
gullf'ren' - girlfriend
gwi' - going
gwine - going to
haa'd - hard
haa'm - harm
hab - have
han' - hand

Glossary

heah - here, hear
hep - help
huccome - why (how come)
huh - her
jes - just
'kase - because
kin - can
kinfoke - kinfolk
kyarrysene - kerosene
lak - like
Lawd - Lord
Lawd hab mussy - Lord have
  mercy
leetle - little
leh - let
letly - lately
lib - live
liss'n - listen
lub - love
madduh - matter
Maussuh - Master
mebbe - maybe
mek - make
'membuh - remember
nat'ral - naturally
Nawt' - North
nebbuh - never
nutt'n' - nothing
nyuse'tuh -used to
obuh - over
odduh - other
'ooman - woman, women
oonuh - you
onduh - under
oshtuh - oyster
pit - put
plat-eye - an apparition
rudduh - rather
saa'f - soft
sef - self

sence - since
sodjuh - soldier
shawt - short
sho - sure
silbuh - silver
soke - soak
staa't - start
sto' - store
suh - sir
summuh - summer
sump'n' - something
swimp - shrimp
t'ank'e - thank you
tawk - talk
'tell - until
tiah - tire
t'ing - thing
t'ing' - things
t'ru - through
t'ro - throw
tuh - to
tuk - took
tu'n - turn
ub - of
Uh - I
uh - a
waa' - war
waggin - wagon
watuh - water
wawk - walk
weh - where, wear
wid - with
widdin' - wedding
winduh - window
winin' - whining
w'ite - white
wuh - what, that, were
wu'k - work
wuz - was
yaas'suh - yes sir

ABOUT THE AUTHOR:
Young readers have shared the magic of **Idella Bodie**'s imaginative storytelling since the release of her first book in 1971. A native of Ridge Spring, South Carolina, Mrs. Bodie attended Mars Hill Junior College, Columbia College, and the University of South Carolina. She makes frequent appearances at schools and libraries around the state. A former English teacher, mother of four, and grandmother, Mrs. Bodie enjoys a busy life with her husband Jim in Aiken.

Through her delightful literary characters and her colorful images of South Carolina's landscape and historic landmarks, Mrs. Bodie not only entertains but inspires readers of all ages to reclaim the mystery and wonder of childhood.

ABOUT THE ILLUSTRATOR:
Gay Haff Kovach is a freelance illustrator and graphic artist. She is a native of West Columbia, South Carolina, and a graduate of the Ringling School of Art and Design.

Other Idella Bodie books illustrated by Mrs. Kovach include *Ghost in the Capitol, Whopper,* and *Trouble at Star Fort.*